Secret of the Lockkeeper's House

by
Georgia Kohart

Flying
Squirrel
press

FLYING SQUIRREL PRESS

ISBN 0-9706348-2-X

SECRET OF THE LOCKKEEPER'S HOUSE

By Georgia Kohart

Use of cover photos: Tollkeeper's House, courtesy of the Roscoe Village Foundation; Jim the mule and General Harrison canal boat, courtesy of the Ohio Historical Society, Piqua Historical Area.

Printed in the U.S.A.

In loving memory of Margie—my little shadow.

Chapter One

Tessa bounced along on the seat of Bus16, her forehead pressed against the cool window glass. Her best friend, Cassie, sat next to her and chattered on and on, unaware that Tess wasn't paying the slightest bit of attention. They were on their way back to the school from a field trip to the John Paulding Historical Museum.

Tessa twisted a battered gold band around and around her pinkie finger as she looked out the window. Droplets of cold October rain gathered and ran like tears across the window. Her mood was as gray as the clouds that scudded over the flat fields of northwest Ohio. It was hard to believe that school had been back in session for over a month. With each passing day, the bright colors and patterns of her summer memories were beginning to fade and fray like an old, well-used quilt. If it weren't for her cousin, Will having the same memories, she would have thought she was just recalling a vivid dream. But he *had* been there and although he didn't like to talk about it, he remembered everything that happened, too.

Cassie's voice cut into Tessa's thoughts.

"So, I told her that you and I were going to work together on the science project and she got all mad and was like *'well, okay.'* "

Tess responded with an automatic "Oh."

"Well, anyway, so she goes up to the teacher and was telling on us—like we'd done something wrong or something," Cassie said. She turned sideways on the seat to face Tessa. "And Ms. Thomas was like, 'Well, Tiffany, I said to form teams of two, and Tessa and Cassie formed a team of two. You need to find yourself another partner,'" Cassie said, imitating Ms. Thomas, their sixth

1

grade teacher. Taking a brief break for air, Cassie flopped back on the seat and chomped her gum noisily for a few seconds, then continued her story.

"I know Tiffany was mad. She slammed her book down on the desk so hard, I thought sure the teacher was going to say something, but . . ." Cassie chattered on.

Tessa looked down at the ring on her finger and Cassie and Tiffany's spat was forgotten. She had never expected a school field trip to bring such a rush of feelings. She twisted the small gold band with the blue stone around her little finger, as her thoughts drifted to what she had seen shortly before the class had climbed back aboard the big yellow bus for their return trip. She couldn't quit thinking about it and had hardly spoken a word to anyone from that moment. How could something so important be lost on everyone else?

An old, faded patchwork quilt was displayed in a glass case on the museum wall. "And this, children, is a fine example of a mourning quilt," the curator at the museum said as she pointed to the small coverlet behind the glass. "We're very lucky to have it here."

Tessa tilted her head back obediently with the rest of the group and stared at it, bored. Her stomach growled and she wondered how long it would be until they were allowed to eat their pack lunches.

To Tessa it looked like it a fine example of an old ragbag. The scraps of cloth, pieced into a pattern the woman had called "Ohio Star," had paled to the point of almost no color at all. Patches that were once white appeared to have been washed with tea, and bright blues, greens, pinks and yellows were now gray.

Suddenly, Tessa's heart leaped. Staring at the quilt, she heard nothing but the pounding of her own pulse in her ears. She had seen this quilt before. Only it had been new, the colors bright, the stitching tight.

Tessa shook her head. The museum guide was just finishing her speech.

"Today many fine examples of pioneer needlework are unidentified. And although we don't know who made this one or even to whom it belonged, the quilt itself can tell us its story by giving us a few clues. The small size tells us it was a child's quilt. And in a detail that is very unusual, it appears this dark border was added *after* the quilt was completed."

Tessa swallowed hard and looked straight ahead, trying to block out the woman's voice, but it was no use. The words kept coming.

"You will notice down in the lower right hand corner letters and numbers embroidered with thread," the woman pointed out.

"From them we know that the quilt was completed in 1850, which makes it well over 150 years old. It says 'in memory,' which tells us that it a mourning quilt. Does anyone know what 'mourning' is?"

Alex Smith, always ready with a smart answer, muttered under his breath, yet loud enough for the other kids to hear. "Duh, morning is when you get up."

A few snickers rippled through the crowd. The rest of the class, not rude enough to laugh out loud, smiled at his remark.

"Well, yes, morning is when we get up," the woman said, smiling patiently. "But, the mourning I refer to is the time of grief after someone dies. This quilt is in memory of a child. Unfortunately, since most of the lettering has become victim to the passage of time, we don't know the name or age of the child or if it was a boy or girl."

"I hope it was a girl," Alex said, yanking Cassie's hair.

"Ouch!" Cassie yelped.

"Or," the woman said, looking directly at Alex, her eyes glittering darkly, "perhaps it was a *boy.*"

Cassie giggled as Alex squirmed uneasily.

"Now," the curator said briskly, "if you will follow me."

When the rest of the students moved on to the next exhibit, Tessa lagged behind. She wanted to run her hands across the patchwork edged in blue, so neatly sewn with stitches so tiny they were almost invisible—except in one corner, where the stitches made large, wobbly tracks across the quilt. On the opposite corner were the letters and numbers the museum guide had pointed out. But Tessa didn't need to read them. She knew what they said.

"Tess! C'mon" Cassie ran back and grabbed Tessa by the arm. "The bus is loading!"

The bus bumped over a rough spot in the road and Tessa jolted back to the present.

"So, now I don't know if Tiffany is still friends with us or not . . . but, I don't care because . . . " Cassie droned.

Tessa turned part way around in her seat, looking for Will. She scanned the faces in the seats behind the one in which she and Cassie sat and spotted him, sitting alone in the center back seat. Arms folded over his chest, long, thin legs sticking straight out in front and down the aisle, he stared sightlessly at the floor. A muscle just below his left ear jumped as he clenched and unclenched his jaw. Tessa scootched further around and hooked her elbow over the padded seat back. Will's short black hair stood up in spikes where he had run his fingers through it, a habit when he was deep in thought. In the rainy day light, his face was white as blackboard chalk and as expressionless. He looked up. When his dark eyes locked on hers, Tessa knew he'd recognized the quilt, too.

When, on the way back from the field trip, his cousin Tessa turned around searching the faces of the kids in the seats behind her, Will knew she was looking for him. And he knew why. It was because of the quilt. Although it was encased in glass and mounted high up on a wall of the museum, he would have recognized it anywhere. Seeing it there brought a rush of memories that caused a film of sweat to form on his upper lip in spite of the coolness of the day.

Will jammed his hands in the pocket of his hooded sweatshirt, slid further down in the seat and chewed his bottom lip. Busy with the new school year and helping his Dad around the farm, he'd pushed the summer memories away. He'd even managed to convince himself they were just part of a really weird dream. But, how could something as lame as a field trip to a dusty old museum create such powerful reminders? And how could Tess have had the same dream? It wasn't a dream, though. He admitted that now. But who, besides Tess, would believe it? Patrick, his little brother—he'd been there, too—even Patrick thought it had just been a dream. And Will let him. It was just too crazy. Despite loud hoots of laughter from the other kids on the bus, and though he tried to think of something else, the noise faded as Will's thoughts pulled him back to the summer just past, back to the hot July day that started out like any other.

Tessa turned back to the window and gazed through the rain at the wide, still stretch of dark water that ran beside the highway. Jagged black stumps, draped with bright green moss, jutted through the rain-pocked surface of the old Miami and Erie Canal. Her friend's voice faded away as Tessa let herself be drawn back in time, back to summer, then further back—to the summer of 1850.

Chapter Two

A wadded up candy wrapper flew from the back of the bus and over Tessa's head, but she didn't notice. She was lost in thought—thinking about the day last summer when she and her cousins, Will and Patrick, went for a boat ride on the old Miami and Erie Canal and returned forever changed. It happened in July—the best time of year—when it didn't get deep dark until almost until ten o'clock at night. In July the corn was way over her head and coming out in tassel and the water in the pond was clear enough to see the little bluegills that nibbled her toes. And it began in the morning—her favorite time of day—when the air was heavy and sweet as the peaches in the orchard. In the morning, hours stretched ahead full of possibilities, like a pocket of money waiting to be spent.

Tessa poked through the orange tiger lilies that grew around the crumbling walls of the garden shed, looking for the papery, pot-shaped nests of praying mantis. She was supposed to be sweeping out the little building for her mother, but Tessa just couldn't quite make herself pick up the broom.

The garden shed was old. Built of red brick, it had been a real house once, where real people lived. But it hadn't been lived in for over a hundred years. Now the porch sagged dangerously. Inside, the house was full of garden hoses, rakes, shovels and stacks of cracked flowerpots. Big black walnuts and pointy hickory nuts, carried in by mice and squirrels, littered the floor. The ceiling beams of the loft were thick with tubular paper wasp nests. Barn swallows flitted in and out through the broken window glass, building mud cup nests in the corners. But, once upon a time, someone besides wild creatures had called the little brick building home.

Her dad said the small building that served Tessa's family as a storage shed had once been a lockkeeper's house on the old Miami and Erie Canal. The canal, which ran by Tessa's family's farm, had been dug by hand. The spillway from the lock overflow, dry in all but the rainiest springs, had once played an endless concert as the excess water poured in a smooth waterfall around the lock, over the spillway and back into the canal. But by the time the canal was completed in 1845, railroads were already putting the water highway out of business. Since there was no money from tolls to pay for repairs, it wasn't long before canal embankments began to leak and collapse. Then mud and plants narrowed the canal that had once been 40 feet across and at least four feet deep. Now the water hardly ever came over the tops of Tessa's chore boots.

The lockkeeper's job was to operate the lock for boats traveling up and down the canal. Hundreds of locks like the one here had worked as water elevators, lifting and lowering canal boats so they could travel from Lake Erie to the Ohio River. Locks were like water stair steps. Day or night, the approach of a canal boat—cargo or passenger packet—meant that there was a job to be done. When a boat "locked through," it meant the team of horses or mules would have to be unhitched from the towrope and walked further down the towpath to the other side of the lock, while the lockkeeper and crew members from the boat helped open and close the gates. For boats going north toward Defiance, Independence, Providence and Toledo, Lock 32 lowered the boat. For those traveling southward, the lock raised the boat to the next higher level of the canal. About halfway on the Miami and Erie was the Loramie Summit, the highest point on the canal. From there the canal descended south to Cincinnati on the Ohio River and north to Lake Erie. To Tessa, her family's farm was just home. She didn't often think much about the old canal and that it was once a part of the system of transportation that crisscrossed Ohio in the early days, opening the way to America's west.

Tessa gave up on insect hunting and picked up the broom. She sighed. Tessa didn't mind most chores as long as it meant being outside. She enjoyed caring for her 4-H chickens and rabbits. She could work an entire day, building a fort up in the barn loft, climbing up and down the ladder with boards and other supplies probably a hundred times. She and Will often packed a lunch and explored the woods for hours at a time. She loved to help when her dad and Uncle Glen, Will's dad, baled hay and straw. It was a sticky, itchy job, done during the hottest part of the summer. But, teamed up with her cousin Will, Tessa could stack bales from the time the dew dried on the sweet-smelling rows of mown grass or golden-yellow wheat stubble until the sun climbed high overhead at noon. That was when her empty stomach and Dad cutting the motor to the tractor signaled lunchtime. Although they would be absolutely starving, Tessa and Will usually took time to dip in the big pond that nestled in a hollow between their farms and rinse away the dust and scratchy bits of wheat chaff stuck to their sweaty arms, necks and faces.

So, it wasn't always the size of the job that caused her to balk like old Rutherford, one of the family's pet goats, when her mother told her to "buckle down and get to it." It was more a matter of interest. Tessa began to sweep lazily, the dirt swirling around her ankles only to settle back down onto the floor. Then she gave up completely and sank down onto a pile of potting soil bags, lost in thought.

Erie, her big, black tomcat with white whiskers and a little goatee of white on his chin, slowly rose from the patch of sunshine in which he was napping and stretched. He was named for the old canal. Starting with his front paws, Erie reached out and stretched, first with the right leg, then the left, ending with his back left. He stretched so hard, his toes spread wide and shook with the effort. A deep, rumbly purring could be heard from across the room. He strolled over to Tessa and despite his size, jumped as lightly as a kitten onto her lap, curled up and continued his nap.

"I wonder what it was like back then, Erie?" Tessa said aloud, as she stroked the cat's velvety ears. He merely twitched one white whisker in reply. The girl stared out the open window at the neat rows of corn and soybeans, their leaves a bright, rainforest green. The July sun was blinding compared to the cool dark inside the shed. Tessa squinted at the glare and looked down at the sleeping cat on her lap.

"It's hard to imagine that it was all covered with huge, tall trees and knee-deep in dark water instead of farmland," Tessa said. Erie replied with a soft *pur-r-rp* and drifted back to sleep.

For thousands of years the massive trunks of oak, beech, elm, ash, locust, sycamore and hickory trees reached skyward, their branches interlocking to create a dense leaf canopy over a hundred miles long and half as wide. During the growing season it was dusk all the time in the Great Black Swamp. It was not easy to turn the swamp into farms, because not only were there the giant trees and only hand held axes and saws with which to conquer them, the area stayed under water and swarming with mosquitoes for most of the year. But the pioneers went about clearing the land with grit and determination. From the time the first rough cabin, built from the massive logs hewed from the towering giants, rose in a clearing hacked from the darkness, it was less than a century before forests that once blocked out sunlight for miles were only a legend. Once the vast forests were logged out and the boggy land drained, the Great Black Swamp was transformed, for underneath lay some of the most fertile farmland in the United States.

Hearing Margie rustling around in the tiger lilies, Tessa stood and gently set Erie on the potting soil bag where he curled himself nose to tail and resumed his nap.

"What are you up to now?" Tessa said, stepping outside. The dog ran out from under the flowers, panting, her nose frosted with dirt.

"I hope you didn't stir up a rabbit's nest again!" Tessa said.

Kneeling down, she parted the lilies along the wall and saw that a brick had been knocked loose. The rows of handmade bricks lay in a fairly straight line, except for this spot where it appeared as if one had been dug out and replaced. A larger gap had resulted and it appeared as if it had never been repaired. Using a rusty garden trowel, Tessa poked at it. Weakened by age and weather, the remaining mortar had eroded, and the brick was very loose. As the curious young girl jabbed at it with the sharp point of the garden tool, the mortar gave way and the brick thumped to the ground. Sand and pebbles poured out of the hole in the wall. Suddenly, the sun caught an object as it rolled out of the opening. Rainbows of light flashed from it as it tumbled out into the bright sunshine. Assisted by Margie, Tessa sorted through the small pile of rubble that had collected on the grass.

"Hey, get your nose out of there," she said, gently pushing the little black and white spotted dog away.

Margie sniffed and sat on her plump behind, her head tipped and one ear flipped inside out. Her bottom wiggled as her stubby tail wagged rapidly side to side.

Tessa carefully sifted through the small hill of old cement until she unearthed the sparkling object. It was a circlet of gold— a ring. A ring centered with a tiny, dark stone. Clutching it tightly in her fist, Tessa leaned back into the shade against the mossy north wall of the brick structure. She slid down and sat, stretching her legs straight out, her top half in shade and from the knees down in sunshine. The coolness of the worn bricks felt good through her tee shirt on such a hot day. She held the ring out, away from the darkness next to the building and into the light, for a better look. It was blackened, but it appeared to be covered in dirt, not tarnish. She polished it on the front of her shirt, and as the years of grime were rubbed away, the ring began to gleam.

"Hey," she said to the dog, "I think this is real gold!"

Margie let out a little yip and pushed her nose under her mistress' elbow, as if to get a better look at the piece of jewelry cupped in Tessa's hand. Wishing to get a better look herself, Tessa held the ring up to the sun. A blue light, as pure and clear as the summer sky just after sunset, shot from the tiny inset stone.

"Wow," the girl breathed, "this is beautiful."

She tried it on the ring finger of her right hand, but the piece of jewelry would not budge past the first knuckle.

"Darn!"

She tried it on her pinkie and it slid easily in place. Tessa stood with the sun beating down on her head of coppery curls, held her hand out and turned it this way and that while admiring the play of light as it danced over the yellow metal.

"Tess! Tessa!" She heard her mother call.

Tessa looked up to see her mother as she walked down the long slope of the back yard, a dishtowel in her hand.

As her mother neared, Tessa's hand flew behind her back. It wasn't that she wanted to hide anything. She just wanted to keep her little treasure all to herself for a bit longer. She wanted to show it to Will before she showed the mysterious ring to anyone else.

"Are you all finished sweeping out here?" Mary Hudson asked.

Barking, Margie ran up to Tessa's mother, who knelt down and patted the dog's head. Margie panted happily with her tongue lolling out the side of her mouth.

When her mother bent over to pet Margie, Tessa slipped the ring off her finger and into the pocket of her shorts. Now her hand rested atop the faded denim, where she could feel the round outline of the metal through the fabric.

"What have you been up to out here, Margie? Helping Tess get her chores done?" Tessa's mother asked the little dog.

"You know you can't go down and play with Will and Patrick until that building is swept out," she said. "If you would just buckle down and do it, you could have it finished in no time at all. I know you would much rather be at your cousins' messing around with that boat of theirs, but you have to finish your work first."

"I know, I know," Tessa admitted. "Why do we have to get this old shed cleaned out anyway?" Tessa jerked her head in the direction of the building and a note of frustration crept into her voice.

The ring lay heavily in her pocket and all she could think about was hurrying down the road to her Uncle Glen and Aunt Sue's place to show it to her cousin Will.

"You know why," her mother said in the tone that Tessa knew meant she was getting close to trouble. "The garden club tour is next week, and I want to have everything spiffy around here. Now quit stalling around and get it finished up so you can go."

When Tessa's mother turned and marched back up to the house, Tessa could tell that she had pushed her mother far enough. Her mom was a lot a fun most of the time, but when there was work to be done, she was all business.

Tessa Hudson was the youngest of three girls and the only one still at home. Her oldest sister was married and lived in Indiana where she and her husband were high school teachers. Her next oldest sister was still in college, where she was studying to be a park ranger. She was spending her summer planting tree seedlings at a national park in the mountains of North Carolina. That left just Tessa to help out around the farm. Or, as she put it when she was feeling dramatic—forced child labor. She wished everybody would make up their minds. One minute her parents treated her like she was still a baby, the next they expected her to finish her regular chores, plus all the work her sisters did when they were home. And living on a farm meant there was always something that needed to be done, from cleaning the used bedding out of the chicken pen and hauling it out to the compost heap to washing the country dust off her dad's pickup truck.

With the possibility of an exciting mystery tucked in her pocket, a small task like sweeping out a building suddenly loomed larger and even more mountainously boring than before the circle of gold with the shining blue stone fell from its hiding place. Tessa took the ring from her pocket and put it on again. Whose was it? It was so small, it must have belonged to a little girl, Tessa mused.

She just had to get down to Will's! He'd probably say she'd gotten the ring out of a gumball machine, but at the same time she knew he'd be curious about its history. He was a real history buff. His room practically bulged with collections of all kinds: arrowheads and fossils and old tools and postcards. He probably had every *National Geographic* ever published. But, she would never get there mooning around here. Determined to get her chores over with so she could be on her way with her discovery, Tessa picked up the broom and pushed it with renewed energy while her mind stayed on the piece of jewelry that sparkled on her finger. How did it get into the wall of the lockkeeper's house? And how long had it been there? Tessa grabbed the broom and soon clouds of dirt and leaves billowed out the door of the old lockkeeper's house. Erie slipped out in search of a quieter spot.

Chapter Three

"Patrick! You have to lift it higher than that!" The side of Will Hudson's face was smashed against the flat end of a small aluminum boat as he and his 8-year-old brother tried to carry it across the barnyard.

"I . . . am!" The younger boy grunted as he hefted the prow of the craft.

The two struggled through the open double doors of the barn and half carried, half dragged the boat through the small stones of the driveway, one corner digging a deep groove through the pale gray stones. It was a johnboat—made of aluminum and square on both ends. Its once smooth sides and bottom sported a lot of dents. It was the type of boat that gets a lot of wear and tear from being hauled from one fishing spot to another.

Patrick continued shuffling along, but turned his head over his shoulder and eyed the trail they were leaving.

"We better get that raked up before Dad sees it," he told his brother.

"Yeah, okay. Let's get this thing into the canal and then I'll worry about that," Will said.

"You know how mad he gets when we mess stuff up," Patrick continued.

"Okay, okay," Will puffed. "I'll . . . ouch!" He yelped as he tripped over a hump in the grass and banged his chin on the hull.

He dropped the boat in disgust. Patrick, unable to handle his end of the load alone, did the same. Breathing hard, they sat on the upside down boat to rest. Its new paint job, while not very neat, glowed fresh and white in the afternoon sun.

Will swiped at his sweaty face with a forearm, spreading a smear of dirt down one side.

"Hey," Patrick piped, "you've got dirt on your face."

"Well, so do you, grandma."

The younger boy worked at his face with the hem of his tee shirt, but since it was equally as dirty, only succeeded in rearranging the smudges on his forehead, chin and cheeks. A matching ring of sweaty grime circled his neck.

"I am going to get this thing into that water today, if it's the last thing I do," Will muttered, staring in the direction of the old Miami and Erie Canal.

"We could ask Dad to help us," Patrick suggested.

"You can call him in out the fields if you want to, but I'm not sticking around to see it," his brother said. "They're calling for thunderstorms tonight and tomorrow. You know that would ruin the wheat, so the last thing he's gonna want to do right now is stop taking off wheat to help us push this tub into the canal. We'll get it but good."

"Okay, but I'm tired and hot and thirsty and . . ." The boy thought a moment before adding to his list of complaints. "And," he said dramatically, "I have . . . one . . . two . . ." His lips moved as he searched the palms of his hands, counting to himself. "I have seven splinters in my hands," he concluded proudly.

"Hey, you're the one who begged to help saw boards for the new seats," Will snapped. "Don't blame your splinters on me. Go on back up to the house if want to."

He was just as tired, thirsty and hungry as Patrick and was positive he had at least as many splinters as his brother, probably more, since he had sawed by hand the old pieces of wood he found in the barn to make new seats for the boat. But he wasn't about to admit it to himself or anyone else before he reached his goal. The boat was going into the canal. He'd worked too long and too hard to give up now.

Head down, Patrick trudged up to the house, dragging the toes of his sneakers through the gravel. Will, with his back turned, listened until he heard the opening squeak, followed by the slam, of the screened back door.

A light breeze played across the barnyard and rustled the leaves on the tall cottonwood tree whose limbs stretched over the circle of lawn, casting shade over that entire corner of the barn. It was the original barn on the property, painted oxblood red. Although it was still in good shape, it was built when farmers still relied on mules and horses instead of tractors. It was too small to house the majority of large equipment—the disks and combines were stored in a long metal pole barn.

Will grabbed the ball cap off his head and combed his fingers through his short, dark hair until it stuck up in damp little spikes. He was thirsty, but it was a long walk up to the house. His mother didn't like for him to drink the water out of the spigot in the barn, fearing it might not be safe, but he gave serious consideration to sneaking one anyway. It had to be pushing 90 degrees, he thought. But it was much cooler in the shifting, dappled shade of the cottonwood. Deciding not to make the trek to the kitchen, he slid down onto the dry grass and leaned his back against the cool aluminum hull of the boat and looked up through the limbs of the tree.

The little hanging pouch of a bird's nest dangled from a slender branch almost directly overhead. All spring the orioles' loud, cheerful notes had sounded over the farm, and Will had seen a flash or two of orange wings. But it was only now, from this position, that he had finally been able to see the nest. While he watched, one of the parents approached and the high, thin cries of hungry babies could be heard coming from the woven grass pocket.

A steady sound like a giant vacuum cleaner came from a distance. His dad was at the wheel of the big silvery-gray Gleaner combine, taking off wheat in the field that stretched from the far side of the canal back to the woods. Uncle Brent waited in the semi, its trailer already half full of pale golden grain. If they finished up today and the rain held off, Will and Tess would be soon be helping stack bales of clean, golden straw left behind when the wheat was harvested.

Gone were the days of plows pulled by mules and cows milked by hand. Like everything else, farming was computerized. But it still meant a lot of lifting and shoveling. And a farmer also had to be a good mechanic, electrician and a have a head for business. If raising livestock, a farmer had to know as much as a veterinarian. Will didn't know if he wanted to go to college to major in agriculture or history. He loved both.

He did know he couldn't wait until he was 14 and allowed to drive the big orange Allis-Chalmers tractor. Some kids he knew, and a lot younger than he was, too, were allowed to drive their family's tractors. It was embarrassing to be treated like a little kid. But Will's parents could not be budged on that rule, no matter how much he reasoned or begged. Two years was an eternity to wait. For now he had to be content with the riding lawn mower and his 4-wheel ATV. Will gave a little more thought to going to the house for a drink, but didn't move from his comfortable seat under the cool umbrella of cottonwood shade.

Scratching absently at a mosquito bite on his ankle, Will's thoughts drifted to the Miami and Erie Canal. He couldn't wait to get his boat, a treasure he'd spotted at a garage sale down the road, a bargain at $7.50, into the water. He had plugged the few holes in the bottom and along the welded seams with a tube of silicone caulk. When he tested his patching job by pouring buckets of water into the boat, none had leaked out. The true test of his repairs would be if, once underway, any water found its way *in*.

Will wanted to see how far he could go, both up and down the canal. He knew he could get the boat the half-mile down to the old lock at Tessa's, on his Aunt Mary and Uncle Brent's farm, but how far beyond that was a mystery. He and Tess had explored the old canal towpath for a distance on foot—at least three or four miles. But he wasn't sure how far the *Marvelous Miami Mist* would take them, especially at this time of year when the water level was low.

The boat had been set up on two sawhorses in the barn, and Will had been painting it when he and Tess had decided on the name. Tess, seated on a bale of straw, had agreed to do the lettering since she had more patience than Will when it came to that.

"I want to use the word "Miami" in it somehow," Will said as he stepped back to admire his paint job. *Miami Marauder!* Yeah, I like that."

"Uh-uh," Tessa disagreed. "We're not going off to war. This is a peaceful exploration, more of a fact finding mission, not an invasion."

"Oh, for crying out loud, Tess," Will said. "It's just a boat. It doesn't have to *mean* anything."

"Hey, you guys!" Patrick dashed through the double doors, slipped on some loose straw and slid, hands outstretched, toward the boat.

"Pa-a-at-trick!" Will shouted as he attempted to fling his body between the falling boy and the hull of the freshly painted boat.

It was too late. Although Will managed to tackle his brother around the ankles, the force only served to push the younger boy farther forward, pitching him into the sticky wet paint before both tumbled to the barn floor in a tangle of arms, legs and white paint.

Tessa bent over and howled with laughter. "You . . . you . . ." she gasped, pointing at the boys, "that . . . that . . ."

When Patrick managed to free himself and get to his feet, the front of his red tee shirt was a solid sheet of white. Without thinking about the wet paint on the palms of his hands, he tried to brush off the straw that clung to his knees and the seat of his pants. When he brought his hands away, there were white smears all over. Straw stuck to the paint on his face and everywhere else there was wet paint, making him look something like a blond porcupine.

At this, Tessa snorted and collapsed, giggling again, onto a bale of hay.

Without even a glance at his brother, Will crawled over to the boat to inspect the damage. Seeing the perfect imprint of his brother's belly and outstretched palms in the side of the johnboat, the muscles just below his left ear, where the angles of his jaw met, worked and tightened. Still on his knees, his face darker than an approaching storm, he turned toward his brother.

"Patrick," Tessa warned, "I think you'd better get out of here . . ."

Will had been able to paint over most of the evidence of Patrick's accidental slide into home, although, in the right light, it was still possible to make out a faint set of handprints. When the final coat of paint finally dried without another mishap, Tess carefully lettered *Marvelous Miami Mist* on the right front side. She had added the *Mist* to Will's *Miami*. He kind of liked that. It reminded him of ghostly things, like "the mists of time."

In his opinion, the extra word *Marvelous* was stupid and dorky. Mainly he hated it because Patrick thought of it, and Will didn't want him to have any ownership of *his* boat. But Tess convinced Will that if he didn't include his little brother's idea, his feelings would be hurt and he might end up with some complex or something. Tess almost always stuck up for Patrick. She thought he was cute and funny, but to Will, his brother was a scrawny little, freckle-faced pest who never shut up.

Luckily, Will thought, Mom stepped in sometimes and suggested that Patrick find something else to do for a while and leave Will alone. It was then that Will liked to explore up and down the towpath and imagine the days of long ago, when teams of mules had plodded patiently, day and night, pulling the long, low boats along the old canal.

It was hard to believe that the shallow ditch behind the farm had ever been anything more than a home for frogs and cattails. When summers were hot with little rain, the canal dried up, leaving only a few puddles here and there, spongy and lime-green with algae. But Will had done a report on the Miami and Erie Canal in the fourth grade and he learned that a lot of history had happened in his own backyard.

The first spade of dirt on the Ohio canal system was turned by Governor DeWitt Clinton of New York and the governor of Ohio, Jeremiah Morrow, in Newark, Ohio. Many people attended that ceremony on July 4, 1825. It was the beginning of a new, but short, era for the young state of Ohio. At one time, over a thousand miles of canals carried boatloads of people and cargo all over the state.

Thousands of people traveled to the Northwest Territory—to the Ohio Land. Many were Irish and German immigrants who had helped to build the Erie Canal in the state of New York. Their skills and strength were needed to dig and scoop the heavy clay soil and build the hundreds of wooden and stone locks and aqueducts needed to keep the proper level of water in the canals. It must have been a busy place back then.

Will couldn't believe how hard those men must have worked. Farming was hard work, but those guys really had it bad. From the moment the sun rose in the morning until it set in the evening, they worked for a measly 30 cents a day. The workers were given food and a place to sleep, but the meals were too little and not very good and they often slept in a leaky tent or a dirty boarding house. A lot of them got sick and died from diseases like typhoid and malaria. A little bit of whiskey was given to the workers every day in hope that it would help keep malaria away. Just like the food and shelter, the whiskey was usually bad. It might have made the workers happier, but it didn't prevent malaria, the dreaded disease they called "fever and ague." Back then people didn't know mosquitoes were to blame. They didn't know much about germs. They thought illness traveled in the mist that rose from the swamp.

As a result of the poor working conditions, accidents and disease, the canal soon earned the nickname the *Irish Graveyard*. A tiny shiver zipped up Will's spine as he wondered if any of the dead men lay buried beneath his feet.

Will peered across the field that his father and uncle were harvesting. The sun was white hot in the sky, creating waves that twisted in shimmery threads above the bristles of wheat straw left by the Gleaner. Some of the golden dust hanging over the field detached itself and moved toward him. For a moment he thought his eyes were playing tricks, but he realized that it was Barley, his dog.

"Barley!" Will called. "Here, boy!"

The Golden Labrador Retriever's ears perked and he headed toward Will in a loose gallop. He collapsed onto the cool grass, panting.

"You goof! Helping with the farming?" Will scrubbed his fingers into the soft, corn silk colored fur behind Barley's ears. "It's too hot to be running around like that."

Will rested his cheek on the dog's boxy head. It was hot to the touch and carried a faint scent, like baking bread, from the wheat field.

"Hey, buddy," he said. "Do you want a drink?"

Will went to the tall spigot by the barn and filled a large, tan crock with cold water. The dog lapped thirstily then looked up. Water dripped from his muzzle. Will thought sometimes it looked as if Barley were smiling at him. He smiled back and searched around in the pocket of his shorts and brought out a dog biscuit.

"Here you go," he said.

The dog took the treat and returned to his spot under the cottonwood tree. Watching Barley slurp up the fresh water was more than Will and his thirst could stand. He sneaked a look at the house to make sure no one was watching, then put his mouth to the spigot and drank deeply. The animals were watered from the barn well, but Will's mother didn't think it was safe for people and made Will and Patrick go all the way up to the house when they were thirsty. The water at the house came from a different well that connected to a filter system in the basement. But the barn well was deep and the water ran clear and cold, so cold it made his teeth ache. It tasted different, too. Almost sweet, it was full of iron and sulfur and other minerals from far down in the ground.

His mother's two favorite words were "be careful." She worried too much. Will formed a cup with his hands and drank again. Then he splashed a little over his head and joined Barley under the cottonwood. The dog sprawled on the cool grass, sound asleep, his upper lip making a little puff every time he breathed out.

Chapter Four

"Hey, I thought that boat would be in the water by now."

Will started and turned around. Barley sleepily lifted his head and gave a soft "woof" while his broad, heavy tail thumped against the hard earth of the barnyard. Tessa held a couple of cans of soda pop she had brought from home and when she walked, one clanked against the ring in her pocket. She hadn't worn it for fear she might lose it. Will squinted and shaded his eyes against the bright splashes of sunlight that fell through the leaves of the cottonwood as he watched Tessa approach.

"It's about time you got here," he said.

Tessa ignored her cousin. "I had stuff I had to get done first. You did, too. I heard my mom talking to your mom on the phone. Did you finish washing the tractors?"

"I did that early this morning," he said, "probably before you were even up."

Tessa started to protest.

Will held up a hand. "I know. I know. You have to get your beauty sleep."

Tessa responded by pushing her cousin.

"Ouch! Ouch! Ooch! That hurts!" Will fell over, clutching his arm in exaggerated pain. He faked a couple sobs.

Barley barked, dashed over to Will and licked his face.

"Tessa's mean isn't she, boy?" Will said to the dog.

"Oh, shut up! I have something to show you!" Tessa said. She reached into her pocket and held out the ring.

"A ring," Will said, unimpressed. "Now that is really something."

He took the jewelry from Tessa and slipped it on his left pinkie. "Oh, you *shouldn't* have! How did you know this was just

23

what I wanted?" He teased. Then taking the ring off, he held it very close to his eye and pretended to be a jeweler. "I would say this is a very rare piece . . . probably worth millions . . ."

"Will," Tessa said, "I found it . . ."

"In a gum machine?" Will handed the ring back.

"I knew you were going to say that," Tessa said. "No, I found it in the shed, the old lockkeeper's house."

"Yeah, so? Probably one of your sisters dropped it out there or something."

"No, you don't get it," Tessa said. "I found it *in* the house. In the wall. I think it's really old."

Plopping down beside her cousin, Tessa handed him one of the cans. Barley ambled over to Tessa, tail waving. She patted his back and scratched under his chin while the dog blissfully closed his eyes.

Will popped open his soda and took a couple of deep drinks, then eyes bulging, belched loudly.

"Very nice," Tessa said. She swallowed some pop and after a moment let out an even louder burp.

Will shook his head in admiration. "You win. You have got to teach me how you do that."

"It's all in the swallowing," Tessa said proudly. "So, anyway, back to the ring. What do you think?" Tessa asked, "Really. Do you think it's worth anything? I wonder how old it is."

Will looked at the ring a second time. "Well, it's made of a very soft metal," he said, squeezing it gently. I remember reading somewhere that they used to make gold with less stuff added in to make it strong. And gold doesn't tarnish like silver or brass and other metals."

"That's what I thought," Tessa agreed, as Will held the ring up so that the blue gem sparkled. "It's so small it must have belonged to a little girl. It's such a pretty blue stone."

"I wonder if it could be a real sapphire?" Will said. "I don't know much about this kind of stuff. Maybe we could find a book at the library on old rings or jewelry," he suggested, handing the ring back to Tessa.

"I just wonder how it got in between those bricks," she said, putting the ring back into her pocket. "When we get down to my house, I'll show you where I found it."

"Okay," Will said. ""Right now Patrick isn't around, so it's the perfect time to take off!"

"Hey," Tessa said, "We need to have a christening ceremony. People always hit boats with a bottle when they first go in the water." She held up her pop can. "We can use this."

Tilting her head so she could read them better, Tessa gazed at the upside down words on the boat: *Marvelous Miami Mist.* She admired her bright red lettering. Other than a few drips and a couple of smears, it was a pretty good paint job. Tessa still thought Patrick's *Marvelous* added a certain something even though Will had been opposed to his brother's input.

Tessa finished her soda. "I'm still thirsty. I'm going up to the house to get a drink."

"No! Don't do that!" Will said. "Patrick'll find out you're here and want to go with us!"

"So what?"

"I just don't want him to, okay?" Will said. "Get a drink out of the pump by the barn."

"We've never been allowed to drink that water," Tessa said. "It's supposed to be contaminated or something."

"Ah, I drink it all the time," Will said.

Tessa crossed her arms over her chest. "Wasn't there some kind of epidemic or something?"

"It happened ages ago," Will said. "It was like a hundred years ago or something. You'd think people around here would have gotten over that by now."

Although she acted tough around Will, the stories about people dying along the canal still gave her goose bumps—especially on misty nights when the fog, lying like thick quilt batting in the canal, gradually flowed over the banks and crept up toward her house.

She shuddered and said, "Well, thanks, but I'll pass. I'll wait and get a drink when I get back home. How far past the old lock are you planning to go and are you going to row all the way back up here again?"

Will thought for a second. "I don't want to plan everything out. That takes all the fun out of it. Then it's not an adventure. Everything is so predictable around here, I'm going to dry up and blow away with boredom. We'll just have to see how far down the canal we can go. I do know it'll be a lot easier if Patrick doesn't come along."

"Oh, he isn't that much of a bother," Tess said.

"Yes, he is. You always stick up for him!"

"It's just that you're so mean to him. You're the oldest. You don't know what it's like to be the youngest and I do," Tessa said. "Nobody ever takes you seriously. No one wants to hear your ideas. They make fun of you all the time and treat you like a baby."

"Yeah, yeah, yeah," Will said, tipping his head back and tapping the last few drops of pop into his mouth. "Anyway, now that you're here, you can help me get the *Mist* into the water. It's going nowhere fast, sitting here on dry land."

Will and Tessa picked up the battered *Marvelous Miami Mist* without much effort and carried it to the edge of the canal. Barley padded along behind. After struggling up the slight incline, they flipped the boat over. Will took a length of baling twine out of the back pocket of his jean shorts and tied one end to the boat and wrapped the other around a small clump of raspberry canes that jutted out over the water. With a slight push, the boat slid into the water. The *Mist* floated and for the moment, didn't leak. The cousins stood and admired the dented craft as it bobbed gently in the water. Like two marionettes connected by the same string, their heads swiveled as they looked slyly toward the house, back at the boat and then at each other.

"C'mon!" Will leaped lightly into the back of the boat.

Tessa hesitated for only a second and followed, wincing when her flip-flops slapped loudly when she landed in the boat.

"C'mon, Barley!" Will said.

He patted the wooden seat, but the dog hung back.

"Barley," Tessa crooned. "Let's go for a ride."

Uncertain, the dog placed first one, then the other of his big, square paws onto Tessa's seat. She grabbed his collar and with a little tug, the rest of him followed. He settled on the floor between the two seats and rested his chin on the edge. The momentum of Barley's leap pushed the boat to the end of its tether.

"Dang!" Will said, as he pulled the *Mist* back to shore by the rope. "I forgot the oars. We'll have to run and get them out of the barn. I hope they're dry. I painted them last night. Barley, you stay."

Will climbed out and clambered up the side of the embankment while Tessa held the craft steady. She let go of the rope and the *Mist* began to drift to the end of it again.

"Wait!" she called to her cousin. "You're going to have to hold it so I can get out."

"Just stay there," Will called back over his shoulder. "I'll get them. Just take me a second. Keep a lookout for Patrick."

Tessa scootched down onto the flat floor of the boat, hooked her legs up over the seat toward the prow and leaned her elbows on the seat in the back.

"Hey!" Will's voice hissed from somewhere above.

Tess, startled, sat up quickly, her feet banging on the bottom of the boat. It sounded like someone kicking an empty 50-gallon steel drum.

"Ss-ss-sst! He's gonna hear you!"

Looking around for the source of her cousin's voice, Tessa finally saw his face peering from a small open window high up in the barn loft.

She waved and started to stand up when Will stiffly poked a finger in the direction of the house, shook his head warningly and made a hacking motion across his neck.

Patrick was sitting on the back step of the house, sucking on a clear plastic sleeve of frozen juice, his eyes crossed with the effort. He couldn't see Will because the barn window looked to the side, but if Tess stood up, she would be in Patrick's sight.

She quickly ducked back down into the boat. Suddenly, a long, missile-like object shot through the air and hit the ground with a small thud. It bounced, end over end, kicking up little puffs of dust, before falling flat on the grass. Tessa raised up on one elbow and peered over the side of the boat to see what had come flying out of the barn with the sincere hope that it had not been her cousin. With relief, she saw that it was an oar, not Will, lying flat in the grass. Just then another soared through the air and landed with a soft "whump" a few feet away from the first.

If Patrick hadn't noticed the oars flying through the air from his perch on the back step, he wouldn't be able to see them in the grass, either. Tessa hazarded a look at the small boy and saw that he was still engrossed with his frosty snack. She glanced back up at the loft window to see Will flapping and flailing his arms in an effort to communicate. Tessa squinted, trying to figure out what was he was trying to tell her. She had recently learned a little sign language from a book on Helen Keller, but she couldn't decipher just what message Will was trying get across. He repeated the neck-chopping motion, then disappeared from view for a moment. His head reappeared, rising from the bottom sill of the window. Tessa concentrated on his performance. Will pointed down, then pantomimed surprise and discovery and made a pouncing motion. Still completely puzzled, Tessa shook her head and scrunched her shoulders to show she didn't understand.

Frustrated, Will scrubbed at his face with both hands before repeating his performance. He jabbed his finger in Tessa's direction, then down, pretended surprise and discovery again and added the motion of holding something long in both hands, followed by a repeat of the downward pointing.

Tessa pointed uncertainly at herself and Will responded with enthusiastic nodding. Quickly peeking at the house to make sure that Patrick was still occupied, she then looked back to the barn window. It was empty. Suddenly, Will was visible again as he pantomimed paddling an imaginary canoe across the opening. He floated out of sight, then reappeared wearing a hopeful expression.

Comprehension dawned on Tessa and she grinned and nodded. Will wanted her to get the oars! She hurried over and picked them up just as a thin voice drifted from up by the house.

"Wi-i-ill . . . Te-e-essa . . ." Patrick called.

"Hurry!" Will hissed as he dashed past Tessa, headed for the *Mist*.

Chapter Five

"Okay," Will breathed, as he slipped the steel pegs of the oar-locks into the matching rings on the boat. "We're all set."

Barley's tail thumped in greeting as the boy, still keeping low, settled onto the middle seat and prepared to row.

"Want me to help?" Tessa asked. "There's room for both of us on that seat. We could each take an oar. Make less work that way."

Will shot a scornful glance in Tessa's direction, shoved the oars into the water, brought the handles to his chest and pushed. The boat slowly began to move. The tall green blades of reeds sighed and creaked as the boat pushed through.

"I can do it," he said.

"Well, okay, but you might want to turn around because we're going the wrong direction," Tessa whispered. "My house is that way." She pointed in the opposite direction.

Glaring at his cousin, Will silently pivoted on his seat and grabbed the oars by the handles again.

With his back to Tessa, he muttered, "All right. You might as well take one. We'll go faster that way."

Barley's tail continued to thud loudly on the floor of the boat as Tessa climbed over and joined Will on the center seat. She pushed against the bank with the paddle end of her oar, and the flat nose of the johnboat swung toward the center of the canal. A few strong strokes with the oars pushed them out of the cattails and elderberry bushes that grew along the water's edge.

A wide grin stretched across Will's face as they started to move down the canal and began to pick up speed.

"We did it! We did it!" He said gleefully. "We got away without Patrick!"

Barley panted happily and his thick tail thumped double time at the sound of Will's voice. Each time his tail slammed on the floor of the boat, the sound boomed and the water rippled around the boat. No longer able to contain his excitement, the dog let out a loud "Woorf!"

Will winced. "That did it," he said. "Patrick will find us for sure now."

No sooner did the words leave Will's mouth than the sound of pattering athletic shoes on hard-baked ground could be heard approaching.

"Hey!" Patrick, wearing a puffy orange life preserver, parted the reeds with his hands. "There you are," he panted. "I thought you guys were going to leave without me."

Will felt a flare of anger as his brother waded through the tall, blade-like leaves of the cattails and, clutching at the edge to hold it steady, hopped into the *Mist*. The boat rocked so hard the older two had to grab onto their seats to keep from being tossed into the water.

"Good thing Barley barked, or I never would have found you guys," Patrick said as he settled himself on the small seat in front.

Barley, as if proud of his role in Patrick's discovering the other two, tail still waving, pointed his square muzzle into the air and barked again.

"Yeah, good thing," Will sighed, his shoulders hunched in defeat, his chin in his hand.

"Well," Patrick said, looking around expectantly, "what are we waiting for? Cast off! Let's go!"

"Yeah, cast off." Will repeated sorrowfully, staring ahead, chin still in his palm.

Tessa felt a big bubble of laughter welling up at the sight of Will's face. His lower lip hung out and he scowled so that his dark brows almost covered his eyes. She had seen black thunderclouds that were more cheerful. She swung Will's oar around and poked him with it.

"Come on," she laughed. "It's not that bad. Let's go."

Will silently took the oar into his hands, then sat motionless as he wrestled with his feelings. He was so mad about Patrick; he wanted to climb out of the johnboat and stomp all the way up to his room, slamming doors as he went. But, he decided, he wanted to take the boat down the canal and between the walls of the old lock at Tessa's even more.

Tessa grabbed her oar with both hands and leaned into her rowing. The boat leaped forward.

"Come on, Will," she said. "It'll be okay. Quit feeling sorry for yourself. We'll still have fun."

Shooting a final glare at Patrick, who had no idea he was at the center of his brother's inner battle, Will pulled at his oar and the *Marvelous Miami Mist* floated into the middle of the canal, headed for points south.

"Do you know how ridiculous you look in that life preserver?" he asked his brother irritably. "The water's only about a foot deep here."

"Better safe than sorry, Mom always says," Patrick said, tightening one of the straps.

"Oh, for cryin' out loud . . ." Will muttered.

It only took a few minutes for Tess and Will to settle into a smooth rowing pattern. As the three kids, plus Barley, floated along, the faint, fishy smell of the canal drifted past their noses. The day remained warm and close, but it was much cooler on the water. Dragonflies darted here and there, as if jerked by invisible threads. A horsefly landed briefly on Barley's nose, then, as the dog snapped at it, zoomed off again.

Occasionally, a frog flung itself from the bank with a squeak, and a loud "ploop" sounded as it splashed into the water. Patrick bounced in his seat as he pointed at a red-eared turtle basking in the sun on a jutting branch of a fallen tree. As the *Mist* drew closer to the shelled creature, Barley also took notice. He stood up, his claws screeching on the aluminum of the boat bottom, and barked at it. The turtle silently slipped off the limb and disappeared into the mossy green water the same color as its shell. Overhead the sun grew larger as began its slow trip toward the west.

"How far are we gonna go, Will?" Patrick asked.

"I don't know."

"How far are we gonna go, Tess?" The younger boy asked, turning toward his cousin.

"Well, I'm getting out at our place," she replied. "I don't know how far the *Captain* plans to go," she said as she elbowed Will in the side.

He grinned and shoved her with his shoulder.

"I do know it won't be quite as easy with only one person rowing on the way back," Tessa said, "although what tiny bit of current there is will be in your favor. Of course, you could do it the old-fashioned way and Patrick could tow you with a rope. He could be the mule."

Patrick brightened at this suggestion. "I could be a mule, Will. Just like in canal days! I know I could!"

"I was just kidding, Patrick," Tessa said. Turning around to see how far they had to go, she said, "We're moving along pretty fast. Let's let up a little on the rowing. I'm not in a big hurry, are you guys?"

"I can help row on the way back," Patrick said. "I can do it."

"No, you can't. You're too short," Will said.

"Am not!" Patrick's bottom lip puffed out.

"Cut it out, you guys!" Tessa said sharply.

As she leaned forward to swing her oar out of the water, the ring in her shorts pocket jabbed into her leg. The ring! Resting the oar on the edge of the boat, she took the ring out of her pocket.

"Let me see." Patrick stood up and grabbed for the ring.

Tessa snatched her hand away.

The *Mist* rocked back and forth and water slapped up the sides and sloshed over the edges, down into the boat. Barley's claws screeched as he struggled for balance.

Will sucked air in between his teeth. "Be careful, you guys!"

"Sit down," Tessa said firmly, pushing Patrick back onto his seat.

"Where'd ya get that?" Patrick asked. "Can I see it?"

"Well," Tessa said, "it's kind of old. Maybe I'd just better hold it and let you look at it."

"Ah, c'mon, Tessa," Patrick whined. "Lemme see it."

"I wouldn't let him have it," Will said sourly. "He'll probably drop it in the canal."

"Shut up, Will!" Patrick said. "I promise I won't drop it, Tess."

"Oh, all right. Here." Tessa held out the ring. "But be careful." She warned.

"Did you find it in a treasure chest?" Patrick said. "Buried treasure?"

"I guess it was sort of buried," Tess said.

"Wow," Patrick said as he held the circle of gold between his thumb and forefinger and squinted at it. "I bet it's worth a million dollars."

"I don't know if it's worth much, but Will thinks it might be real gold," she said. "See how it's shiny and not tarnished?"

"Where did you say you found it?" Will asked. "In that old house?"

"It was stuck between the bricks, outside. I was poking at a soft spot where it was crumbly and it just sort of fell out."

"I want to see it," Patrick whined when Will plucked the ring from his hand.

"Here," Tessa said, taking the ring from Will and handing it back to Patrick. "Look at it and then let me put it back in my pocket where it'll be safe. I don't want to take any more chances. With you two in the same boat, we'll be lucky if we don't all wind up walking the rest of the way to my house!"

Patrick glanced at the ring, then handed it back to his cousin, more interested in having his turn than in the jewelry. Tessa pocketed it and picked up her oar.

"You know," she said, "next time I ought to bring Margie. I think she would like this."

"Oh, yeah, that's just what we need," Will said, "another dog along for the ride."

"She wouldn't take up any room at all," Tessa said, slightly offended. "I don't see why Barley can and she can't."

"Yeah, Will." Patrick said. "I *like* Margie."

Tessa whirled to stare at Will. "Don't you like Margie?"

"I never said I didn't like your dog."

"Oh, yes he did," Patrick said. "He said she yaps a lot."

"Well," Will said in self-defense, "she does yap a lot. You said so yourself, Tess. But I never, ever said I didn't like her, Patrick."

"Patrick, why do you do that?" Tessa asked.

"Do what?"

"You know what."

"What?" He asked innocently.

"You know what I'm talking about, taking things Will says and trying to twist them around into something that'll make me mad," Tessa replied.

"Huh?"

"Okay, okay," Will interrupted. "Margie is welcome to come along any time she wants."

In no time at all, the group had traveled the mile between the two Hudson farms. As they approached Tessa's, they could see the outbuildings of the farm on the right. As they glided by the barn, she thought how different it looked from that point of view, rather than the one she had seen every day of her life.

As the smooth stone walls of the canal lock came into view, Tessa's dog, Margie, dashed barking up to the edge of the canal.

Barley leaped to his feet with a low growl, then recognized his little spotted playmate and answered with several barks of his own. Margie zipped back and forth beside the canal, yapping crazily.

"Margie! Hey, Margie! It's me!" Tessa shouted.

The little terrier didn't pay any attention to Tessa's calls. Like a black and white bullet, she sped ahead then circled back, stopping just long enough to aim another series of sharp barks at the *Marvelous Miami Mist* before taking off again.

"Maybe it's because she's not used to seeing anyone or anything in the canal," Tessa said, wondering about her dog's strange behavior.

"Where do you want to get out?" Will asked Tessa.

"I want to go through the lock. I'll get out on the other side."

Suddenly, Barley's happy barks turned to an uneasy whining. He tried to climb out, causing the boat to tip far over to the side. Patrick reached for the big Lab's collar, but it was too late. With a mighty lunge, Barley leaped from the boat and splashed into the canal. He waded ashore and shook the excess water from his heavy, golden coat. Drops flew through the air, were caught in the rays of the setting sun and fell to earth in a shower of rainbows.

Chapter Six

Barley scrambled up the bank and joined Margie. Then the dogs raced to the top of the old canal lock and stood on the thick wall, barking furiously down at the *Marvelous Miami Mist* as it drew closer and closer to the lock.

"What in the heck is wrong with them?" Will asked.

"I don't know," Tessa said, looking up at the dogs. "I've never seen Margie act like this before."

"I only heard Barley bark like that one time," Patrick said. "The night that guy ran over our mailbox, and he walked up the lane to our house to call for help."

Patrick thought for a moment while the barking became even more frantic. The 12-foot high walls of the lock loomed above them as the boat, rowed by Will and Tess, slowly moved closer. Cool, damp air breathed through the open ends of the 15-foot-wide, 90-foot-long lock chamber. Although it was open to the sky, the long, narrow stretch of stone, with a floor of water, made it feel like they were entering a tunnel.

Margie and Barley leaned over the wall, and barked down at the boat.

"Wait a minute," Patrick said. "Hey, Will? Remember that time Dad tried to catch the raccoon that got into the attic? Barley barked like crazy."

"Yeah, he did go pretty nuts that night," the older boy agreed, his eyes still on the dogs. Then he laughed. "So did Dad."

Tessa smiled too, as she recalled the story of Uncle Glen's wild chase around and around the attic that ended up with the raccoon turning tail and going after him.

"Hey, listen to my voice," Patrick said. "It sounds like we're in a cave! Listen! H-o-o-oo!"

"*H-o-o-oo...*" the sound echoed off the walls.

"Hoo-ooot!" Patrick's whoops joined with the dogs' as they barked down into the lock. Trapped between the thick walls, it created a deafening racket.

As the *Mist* entered the old lock, the dogs' frantic barking turned to howls that blended with Patrick's happy hoots.

"Jeez," Will said as a shiver slithered up his spine, "that gives me the willies!"

Tessa squinted up at Margie and Barley, whose noses were pointed skyward as they gave themselves over to the mournful sound.

"It really creeps me out," she said. "I wonder what's wrong."

"Woo-ho-oo . . ." Patrick stopped suddenly in mid-hoot and his voice dropped to a whisper. "Will."

"*Will,*" he repeated.

Neither Will nor Tessa heard Patrick over the din of the dogs, now almost directly overhead, atop the west wall. Margie was so close to the edge, Tessa could look up and see the pink pads of her feet. A little avalanche of dirt and pebbles worked loose by the dancing paws of the excited dog, trickled down the wall and splashed into the canal.

"*Will.*" Patrick's voice came small from the front of the boat. "Wi-ll?" His voice climbed up the scale until it was a mere squeak.

He was staring, wide-eyed over the edge of the *Mist.* His summer-tanned cheeks had drained of color and his hand waved wildly in the air, trying to catch at his brother's arm.

"Will!" he cried.

Will heard the note of fear in his brother's voice and turned away from the wailing dogs. Tessa heard it, too, and tore her eyes from Margie to see what was scaring Patrick. Even before he could explain what was frightening him, Will and Tessa saw the cause of Patrick's alarm.

The water level in the lock was rising. Rising rapidly. The little johnboat and its crew were quickly gaining altitude as the tide of the canal pushed upward. Caught in a small whirlpool, the *Mist* began turning in what, at first, was an easy circle. The children froze to their seats, as the boat began to spin faster and faster. Tessa and Will, their oars forgotten, clutched the aluminum sides as the boat's spinning increased in speed. Patrick dropped to the bottom of the boat, his eyes squeezed tightly shut. The dogs' cries faded away. The only sound was rushing water as it lifted the *Marvelous Miami Mist* higher and higher and whirled the boat around and around, faster and faster. The three cousins were silent except for an occasional ragged gasp from Patrick. Will closed his eyes to shut out the dizziness.

The water rose higher and higher, climbing steadily up the walls of lock, raising the *Marvelous Miami Mist* and its helpless passengers until they were almost level with the top of the walls. As if from a very long distance, they heard a faint, sad sound, like the moan of a horn.

Hooo-ooot . . . But this time it didn't come from Patrick. And another sound—a man's voice, singing musically up and down, chimed in with the horn.

"Hey . . . lo-ock . . ."

Ooo-ooo-ooo.

"Hey . . . lo-ock . . ."

Hoo-oot. . .

"He-ey . . . lo-o-o-ock . . ."

Hoo-oot. . .

The calls and the horn died away and just as the water reached the top of the lock, the boat finally stopped its wild rotation. Patrick groaned from the floor, his eyes still closed.

"Will . . . I don't feel so good," he said weakly. "I'm woozy."

Will, sensing that the boat had finally come to rest, opened his eyes and sat up. He swayed dizzily. Speechlessly, he nudged Tessa. She slid her hands from her eyes and gasped.

Chapter Seven

Over 150 years ago, the Miami and Erie Canal boasted 106 lift locks. Each became a water elevator when the heavy wooden gates on both ends were closed. The chamber was filled or emptied, lifting or lowering the boats from one level of the canal to the next. Then the freightliners and passenger packets continued north or south.

The walls of Lock 32, although still standing, showed the tracks of time. When the canal was built, the locks on this stretch of the Miami and Erie Canal had been made of wood, cut from the towering white oaks that grew in the Great Black Swamp. As the years passed, the wood was replaced with stone or concrete. Now vines crept across the walls and moss had painted a thick green line where the water lapped at the sides. Tree roots had worked their way between the cracks and dangled like knobby fingers reaching for the water.

Square oak timbers had once lined the floor of the lock, making it watertight. Like the four stout wooden gates at the ends of the lock, they had long since rotted away. But the strong iron straps that had attached the great gates to the lock were still there.

When the little boat holding Will, Patrick and Tessa floated into old Lock 32, it felt like time slowed and stopped. At least that was how Tess remembered it afterward. When everything finally quit spinning around and around, Will nudged her and she opened her eyes. Her head felt heavy as she swung it toward him. Will stared back at her, mouth open, his dark eyes wide.

Patrick still huddled at their feet, his bottom in the air, arms crossed over his eyes. Barley and Margie's barking was silenced. They were gone.

A bubble of fear rose in her chest and Tess sprang up, but plopped back onto the floor. She thought she'd tripped over Patrick, but as she looked down her breath snagged in her throat. Although Patrick was still curled in a tight ball at her feet, he hadn't caused her fall. She'd stubbed her toe on a large coil of dirty rope. Beside it was a stack of small wooden kegs.

Tess slowly raised her head to find Will still staring at her with the same stunned expression. His mouth formed words, but no sound passed his lips. He flipped his hands in tight arcs, motioning for Tessa to look around. She closed her eyes for just a moment for fear of what she might see, opened them and looked around, then promptly squinched them shut again.

Patrick's soft whimpering came to her through the darkness and snapped her out of her shock. She bent over and helped the boy to his feet. His face was slightly greenish and smudged with dirt. He looked up at her, and a tear slid down his pale face.

"Tessa," he whispered, his lower lip quivering, "I don't feel so good."

She picked up the hem of her checked apron and wiped her little cousin's face. Her apron? She was wearing an apron! And under it was a dress, a full-skirted dress that billowed out and hung almost to her ankles. Now Tessa was the one who felt slightly green. The world tilted, and she sank dizzily onto the coil of rope and put her head between her knees. She jolted upright. Gone were her favorite flowered flip-flops! She grabbed the hem of the skirt and pulled it up to her knees. Her legs were still there, but they were hidden in long, white ruffled pants, and on her feet were skinny black boots with lots of tiny black buttons running up the side.

Tessa wanted for it all to go away—to wake from this crazy dream. She put her hands to her head as if to shake some sense into it, only to find a bonnet perched there. She gingerly followed the satiny ribbons from the hat to where they tied under her chin in a big floppy bow. I must look like Bo-Peep, she thought.

Hands still at her neck, she jerked around as from behind Patrick's soft sobs were drowned out by a tight, high-pitched sound. It came from Will, who was pointing at her with one hand and hanging onto Patrick's shoulder with the other. He bent over and shook, all the while emitting odd little noises like one of Margie's squeaky toys.

"Hee-e, Eee-e," he gasped. "Hee-ee."

Alarm washed over Tessa once again, but faded quickly into relief when she realized that Will was laughing. But he was laughing at her! She couldn't believe it. In a matter of seconds, their entire world had turned upside down, backwards and inside out and Will had come down with an attack of the giggles. Even Patrick, whose face had lost its notebook paper whiteness, was snickering. She had never heard Will laugh like that. Seeing tears run down his face, she wondered if he was edging closer to crying.

It was Tessa's turn to stare now, for both Will and Patrick were wearing different clothes, too. Will's baseball cap had been replaced with a battered, round brown hat, its broken brim flopping over his forehead. Not only that, but he wore an odd little jacket and pants that fell halfway between his knees and the scuffed black, ankle-high boots that had replaced his sneakers. In place of Patrick's tee shirt was a long, full shirt with a wide collar. Patrick no longer wore shorts, either, but a baggy pair of pants cut off just below his knees. He wore boots like Will's. If she hadn't been so terrified, Tessa, too, would have burst out laughing. She stamped her foot at Will and instead of the dull metal of the johnboat, it struck a floor made of sturdy wooden planks.

Elizabeth looked down at her feet, then up at Will and Patrick. Their faces stilled. They straightened, and like Tessa, turned slowly around surveying their surroundings. The children stood on the deck of a long, wooden boat. They were in a small open area, a walkway created between stacks of wooden barrels, boxes and crates. Tessa and Will could see over the top of the lock, and everything familiar was gone except the little brick house by the canal.

Suddenly everything came noisily to life.

"Hoo-ooo-ooot!" A horn moaned over their heads.

"Hey-ey-ey, lock!"

A man's voice rang out and all three kids turned at the same time and looked upward, toward the sound. At the back of the boat, on top of what looked like a little wooden house, a man leaned on a large, long tiller. He was looking ahead, to what lay at the front of the long, low boat. He was intent on his work, but sensing the three staring up at him, he looked down and grinned.

"What's the matter? You act like you ain't never seen the Cap'n afore," he said, still grinning. "You been right here on the

Dolley Madison all the way from Piqua and you's all three standin' there, starin' like three owls on a limb." He lifted his battered hat and made a big show of feeling around in his sandy brown hair. "Am I growin' horns or somethin'?"

Tessa looked wildly at Will, whose mouth snapped shut. Patrick's head was still tilted back to stare at the man, but his eyes grew wide and a couple of tears slipped from the outer corners of his eyes and made pale, wet streaks in the dirt on his cheeks as they traveled toward his ears. Without taking his eyes from the man, he dashed them away with the back of his equally dirty hand. Tessa felt her knees weaken again, but she fought the shakiness and grabbed Will's arm.

"What is going on here," she whispered through gritted teeth. "Please pinch me and wake me up!"

"Yeah, well, when we're all done waking you up, better start on me," he muttered grimly. "I don't . . ."

The captain clamped the hat back on his head, chuckling. "Well, you owls will have to excuse me while I take Miz Madison through the lock."

"Headway! Get to that deadeye, boy-o!" The captain shouted and a sudden flurry of activity erupted at the front of the boat. "Hey, Brennan!"

"Aye," a deep voice called out from beside the canal. Brennan was leading a team of sturdy mules along the towpath. He was a big, broad-shouldered man, with black hair that hung nearly to his shoulders from under a shapeless hat. Two teeth were missing from his wide mouth, leaving an equal number of gaps as black as his hair.

A long rope ran from the mule team to the boat and it reeled out behind as they walked on past the lock. Without taking his eyes off the path, Brennan spit a brown stream of tobacco juice into the water with a quick, sideways twist of his mouth.

"Get 'er snubbed up there, Adam," he yelled.

Tessa, Will and Patrick scrambled over crates and around barrels to see what was happening.

Adam, leaning over the front of the boat, gave an answering wave of his hand without looking up. He untied a thick rope from a heavy iron ring. Then he leaped lightly off the boat as it slid smoothly into the lock. Taking up a shorter length of rope attached to the boat, he quickly wrapped it around a short, squat post sticking out of the ground. More of the same heavy rope had been wound around and around into long half-moon shaped bumpers that hung on each side of the prow and protected the boat as it bumped against the sides of the narrow lock.

"Will! Tessa!" Patrick called as he ran to the side of the boat, pointing to the mules passing by. "Horses," he breathed happily.

"Hey, Will," yelled Brennan. "Get up there! Make yerself useful and grab that other bow line."

Will hesitated for a moment, quickly looking behind, checking to make sure that he was the Will to whom the man had spoken. When Will looked questioningly at Tessa, she shrugged as if to say: *"I don't know!"*

"Hey-yup, boy! Look lively!" Brennan made a swirling motion with his hand. "Ye got cobs in yer ears, boy? Snub 'er up, there! Make 'er snug!"

Will didn't know what the guy expected him to do. Another burst of laughter came from the captain.

"Ah, Brennan," he said, "I'll not have you a-barkin' and a-worryin' at the boy's very heels like a mad dog." Each time the captain said a word with the letter "r" in it, it was as if his tongue didn't want to let go of it as soon as the other letters of the alphabet. It sounded like he said bar-r-r-k and wor-r-r-ry.

"Eh!" Brennan called from the path where he stood, gently patting one of the mules. "He's doin' a girl's job of it, I'll wager. Now, Adam, he's a bowsman, all right." The man nodded at the tall boy.

At Brennan's words about "a girl's job," Tessa frowned and whirled to stare at him. Then, following the other boy's example, she leaped off her side of the boat. Copying Adam, she grabbed the rope and busily tugged and twisted the heavy wet line as best as she could around the post. She winced as the rough fibers poked and pricked her hands, but kept at it despite the pain.

Will shot a nervous smile at Brennan, then watched as Tessa got down on her knees, grunting as she wrestled with line. When she stood up, she stumbled awkwardly as she stepped on the hem of her full skirt. Her woven straw bonnet, still tied by its blue ribbon, had fallen down over one eye. She shoved it to the back of her head and wiped her hands on her dress. She blew a loose strand of hair off her sweaty forehead with a puff from her bottom lip and parked her fists on her hips.

"There's a girl's job for you!" she shouted. Her chest rose and fell rapidly, partly because she was out of breath, partly from anger, and partly because she was still scared. Red-faced, Tessa glared at the bearded face.

It was quiet for a moment—the only sounds were the fluttering of one of the mule's lips and the splash of water over the small dam-like structure beside the lock. Suddenly, under his bushy, dark brows, Brennan's eyes twinkled and a roar of laughter erupted from his wide-open mouth. One of the mules pranced around a little and as he turned to calm it, Brennan's shoulders were still shaking.

"Whoa there, Mae. The girl's got spirit. Just like you. That she does."

Tessa wasn't sure she liked being compared to a mule, but the man said it in such a way, she suspected he meant it as a compliment. Will glared out from under brows nearly as dark as Brennan's.

"Thanks for making me look like a complete doof," he growled at Tessa.

"I'm sorry, I didn't mean to," she said. "I . . . I just hate when people say girls can't do stuff just because they're girls!"

"'Tis surely a shame, Cap'n Callahan," Brennan called over his shoulder, "that the young lass is going to be leavin' us so soon."

He said leave so that it sounded like "lave."

"Yer right about that, Brennan," the captain called down. "She maybe would work out better than the new boy-o there," he said, looking down from the roof of the little house on which he stood.

As the captain spoke, Adam turned around. He was tan from hours under the sun and sweat sparkled on the tips of his curly hair. Although quite tall, he was not yet out of his teens. He hurried around to the front of the lock, where the *Dolley Madison's* stern bumped gently against the closed gates.

Captain Tim pushed his hat back and wiped his forehead as he watched the long-legged young man. "That boy-o. I've never seen the likes of a harder workin' one, but never seen one so stingy with his words, neither." He shook his head a little then spoke to Will, Tessa and Patrick. "Well now, young folks, this is your last lock, since you've got to where yer goin' to. You want to ride 'er down, one last time?"

"One last time?" Will asked Tessa. "One last time to do what?"

"And what did he mean by we've got to where we're going?" Tessa said.

"You got me," Will said. "But, here we go."

Chapter Eight

"One last time for what?" Will asked Tessa again. "What's he talking about? I don't remember a first time for anything. Who are these people, and how do they know us?"

Before Tessa could answer, the red-painted door of the little house opened and a woman stepped out, wiping her hands on her apron.

"Tessa, dear," she said, then spotting Will, she said, "Oh, there you are. Why don't you come in the house and freshen up a bit? And you'd best check to see that you've gathered all your things together."

Tessa looked helplessly at Will, as she allowed herself to be led into the cabin.

"Headway!" A man's voice called out.

Will noticed a noise at the front of the lock and headed toward it. As he was making his way around the barrels and boxes on the deck of the long boat, he heard yet another man calling to Adam, who'd leaped off the boat a few minutes earlier.

"Got 'er snubbed up there?" A tall man standing beside the lock shouted to Adam.

Adam answered with a quick nod and a grin.

Then, as if he were winding up a giant toy, the man at the lock began turning an iron crank that stuck up from the top of the gate. As he turned the handle around and around, the *Dolley Madison* began to sink lower and lower in the lock. Will saw that the water level water was lowering and taking the boat with it.

"Will!" Patrick rushed up. "Will! That Brennan guy says I can pet the mules as soon as we lock through!"

"That's nice," Will replied absently, still keeping an eye on the boat's descent.

Patrick hopped up and leaned over the side of the *Dolley Madison*. Looking toward the front of the lock, he yelled happily. "Hey, look! We're goin' down!"

"Yeah," Will said. After all the work everyone had done to get the boat into the lock, he had expected the boat to drop like an elevator, but water level in the lock only went down about six feet.

"Whoa-a-a!" Patrick yelped as he lost his balance and teetered over the side of the boat.

"Patrick!" Will grabbed his brother by his jacket and yanked him back onto the deck. "For cryin' out loud! You could have slipped right over the edge and into the water! If this boat had swung back over, you'd have been smashed like a bug!"

"Oh," Patrick said in a small voice. "I'm sorry. Can I go back over and look at Prudence and Mae?"

"Who?" Will asked shortly.

"Those mules," Patrick said slowly, as if he were explaining to a very small child, "they're sort of like horses. Prudence and Mae are the mules."

"I *know* what a mule is. I just want you stay where I can see you," Will said darkly. "That guy is weird."

"Oh, he just looks mean," Patrick said with an air of wisdom. "Mom always says you can't know everything about a person just by the way he looks. Don't be scared of him."

"I'm not *scared* of him," Will said. "Don't you remember that mom also taught us about not going with strangers? I said stay where I can see you and I mean it!"

"Okay, okay, I will," Patrick said as he headed for two other mules in a small stable on deck.

On top of the two huge lock gates were long beams that stuck out to the side. When the man who had operated the crank pushed on one beam, Adam and Brennan pushed on the other and the gates slowly opened. The ropes holding the boat in place were quickly flipped off the snubbing posts and the *Dolley Madison* floated smoothly out of the lock.

The captain hailed the man at the gate. "Hey there, Hudson! I hear tell I've got some special cargo on board for ye."

A wide smile crossed Hudson's face. "Yeah, it'll be good for the little one to have someone to keep her company other than the likes of canawlers day and night. No offense to you and yours, of course, Callahan."

"None taken, Hudson," Captain Callahan laughed. "I know what you mean. Not all the boats on the Miami and Erie are lucky enough to have a fine woman like me Martha."

As he spoke, Tessa and the woman Will assumed was Martha, left the cabin and came toward him. Tessa carried a small trunk and Martha, who was no taller than Tess, carried a cloth bundle held together with string. She looked unhappy.

"Here are your things, Will," she said, soberly handing the bundle to him. "They're all fresh and clean. Patrick's are in there, too."

When Martha spoke, she smiled at Will and her unlined face brightened from within. Her hair was the brownish-red color of oak leaves in the fall. It was parted in the middle and pulled back over her ears into a knot on the nape of her neck, but a great many curls had worked their way loose and they bounced around like springs with every movement of her head.

"Tim and I are truly going to miss you and little Patrick there," she said nodding in the boy's direction. He was back hanging on the edge of the boat, admiring his new loves, Prudence and Mae. He jigged around impatiently, waiting for his chance to pet them.

"Such a short span of time and already I feel as if you were almost my own," she said, turning back to Will.

Captain Tim came up to the little group and in a falsely gruff voice said, "So, Mrs. Callahan, we're finally goin' to be rid of this mess of characters, especially that troublemaker over there," he said jabbing a thumb in Patrick's direction.

Much to everyone's surprise, Martha emitted a squeak, threw her apron up over her face and rushed back to the cabin and closed the door.

The captain's mouth silently opened and shut several times as he looked first at the closed door and back at Will and Tessa. Giving up his search for words, he followed his wife into the cabin. The two cousins stared at each other, confused over everything that had taken place in the past few minutes. From the little house, painted white and hung with bright blue shutters, they overheard the rumbling of the captain's low voice. A few seconds later both he and Martha came back out, she wearing a weak smile. Her face was blotched with red and her eyes had a watery look about them.

"Well," she said with false cheer to her husband, "I guess we got that speck out of my eye, didn't we?"

Tim looked down at his wife, cleared his throat and nodded. "That we did."

He started to say something else, but from on shore a child's voice piped. "There she is! There she is, Mama! I see her, Papa! That must be Tessa!"

Will wheeled to look at Tessa, who appeared as if she was considering throwing her apron over her own head and making a run for the cabin.

"Hey, there's the family, now," Captain Callahan said. "Yep, we've got 'er for ye, little miss," he called out. Then he tipped his hat and bowed his head slightly at Hudson's wife. "Ma'am."

Martha waved and Mrs. Hudson returned it. The little girl clasped her hands together and held them tightly to her chest.

"Tess," Will whispered, "look at the house by the lock. It's your old brick shed."

Tessa, still staring at the people on the lock, whispered back, "I don't care. I don't want to go with those people."

"Tessa, dear," Martha took her hand and pulled her gently away from Will. "Come meet your new family."

Tessa hung back, but Martha gently urged her toward the family standing on the lock by the little brick house. Watching Tess being led away sent a jolt of alarm up Will's spine and made the hair on his arms rise. He started to go after her, but Tim clamped his big hand on the boy's shoulder.

"I know, I know 'tis hard, me boy-o," he said.

Callahan dug into the deep pocket of his baggy pants and pulled out a thick, folded piece of paper covered with writing. It looked like a bill or something important or official. "I don't know the people who are to come for yerself and Patrick," he said to Will as he looked over the paper. "It don't say anything about you and Patrick, only mentions the girl. I'll wager the Hudsons know what's to be done with ye."

At his words, Martha's face fell. Patrick ambled over and she gathered him into a hug, but he fought to pull free.

"Aw, Martha, you'll smother the child," Captain Callahan said. "Lave 'im be. You'll spoil the child."

Patrick, scowling, broke away and said, "Yeah, Martha, *lave me be!*"

Both Martha and Tim laughed, delighted at Patrick's outburst. Will was too worried about Tessa to take much notice.

"Come on, we might as well go ashore with Tess for a bit, help her make her acquaintances," Captain Tim said. He swung down a short gangplank and motioned for the children to follow. Patrick, eager to finally meet Prudence and Mae face to muzzle, bounced eagerly off the boat. Worried that his brother might get into some sort of trouble, Will followed closely, the cloth parcel in his arms.

Tessa's boot had no sooner touched the ground than the little girl rushed up and grabbed Tessa's free hand with both of her small ones. She was younger than Tessa by two or three years. Her blue eyes, shining out from under the brim of a bonnet decorated with tiny violets, snapped with excitement.

"Tessa! Tessa!" she chanted, jumping up and down. "It's me! It's me, Emaline! Oh, I thought you never *was* going to get here!"

As the little girl pulled her away from the boat, Tessa, her heart pounding, looked desperately over her shoulder at Will. She stumbled, unable to see clearly for the tears that clouded her vision. Will stared helplessly back as Tessa was led away.

As the little girl pulled Tessa away from the boat, she looked desperately over her shoulder at Will. He didn't know what to do, so he stood helplessly still.

"Well, now Hudson," the captain was saying, "what's to be done with couple of lads who know how to earn their keep?"

"Lads?" Hudson said, puzzled. "I don't know anything about any boys. Tessa was the only child of Eva's childhood friend."

Chapter Nine

Tessa lay in the gray light of daybreak in the loft room of the brick house. Outside, a single bird chirped the same note over and over. Just like Tessa, the day was caught in the quiet space between sleep and awake. As she stretched her legs, the ropes under the featherbed mattress creaked.

Emaline Hudson sighed and turned over, rolling herself up in the quilt like a window shade. For as little as she was, Tessa thought, Emaline sure was a bed hog. Every morning Tessa awoke, completely uncovered, lying next to a patchwork covered lump.

She turned on her side and looked out the small window at the pink sky. It was during quiet times like these that Tessa had a chance to think about things. No matter how much she tried, she still didn't know how she, Will and Patrick, simply by taking a rowboat through old Miami and Erie Canal Lock 32, had traveled back in time to 1850. And she didn't know how they would ever get back. Most of the time, like it was all a dream, it just didn't seem to matter. But sometimes she grew homesick for her family, Margie, her dog, and Erie, her cat. Was she missed? Were her parents worried? How much time had really passed? Had she missed the county fair? Maybe it was just a dream from which she'd soon awaken.

Tessa tugged on the quilt and Emaline mumbled something in her sleep and drew the quilt tighter. Tessa yanked again with no luck and gave up trying to regain her share of the quilt. Tessa pulled her toes up under her long, white nightdress to protect them from the early morning chill. More birds were singing now.

It was cool now, but it wouldn't be long before the day became hot and sticky. The thick walls of the lockkeeper's house would hold the July sun at bay until about noon. By late afternoon it would feel like the inside of the beehive oven in which Eva Hudson baked bread. Made of the same heavy Paulding County clay that helped to keep the canal watertight, the brick house held the heat until way after midnight.

At first Tessa had wanted to escape into the coolness of the summer evenings, but the Hudsons wouldn't let her go out after dark. They warned against the night air and the miasma, an invisible cloud thought rise from stagnant pools deep in the Great Black Swamp. People thought it brought disease, especially the one called "fever and ague." Although death didn't always result, a person stricken with the disease suffered from high fevers and bone-rattling chills—the ague. From the way the sickness was described, Tessa thought it sounded a lot like malaria, a disease carried by mosquitoes, not a mysterious swamp cloud.

"Maybe it's the mosquitoes that makes people sick," Tessa said to Eva Hudson one night. "They're thick around here, no matter what time it is, day or night."

Eva Hudson, or Aunt Eva, as Tessa was to call her, simply smiled and told her to come in out of the sun, that Tessa already had too many freckles for a respectable young lady. Stay out of the sun; stay out of the dark. Make up your mind, Tessa thought.

The sun was up now. From far off Tessa heard the sound of a lock horn. Seconds later, she heard the thump of Luke Hudson's sturdy boots as he readied himself for another day of tending Lock 32.

It had been several weeks since the day Tessa had watched Will and Patrick float away, aboard the *Dolley Madison*. As the boat disappeared, so strong was her fear that she would never see her cousins again that Tessa fought the urge to run after it, screaming and waving her arms.

As Tessa recalled that day, it felt as far off and distant as the horn that echoed faintly again from somewhere up the canal.

"So, this is Tessa," Aunt Eva had said kindly, as she stepped up and placed a gloved hand on Tessa's arm. "You are finally arrived. I would know you just from having known your mother when we were girls."

"Tessa is a lovely girl," Martha said, "so pleasant and polite. I'm sure that Emaline will love her right off."

Eva Hudson turned to her husband. "I believe that she strongly favors Sally." Suddenly, a shadow fell over her dark eyes and she looked down so that her bonnet shadowed her face. "We were so sad to hear you were orphaned."

The lockkeeper, Luke Hudson, quickly stepped up and swept his hat from his head. "Welcome to the lockkeeper's house, Tessa. You just call me Uncle Luke. Now perhaps Emaline will give us a rest. She's rushed out for every single packet that's locked through for the past week." With one hand, he grabbed the handle on the end of the trunk and swung it to his shoulder.

Tim Callahan made a throat clearing noise and looked meaningfully at Luke Hudson. When he had the lockkeeper's attention, the captain motioned to him with a nod. The two men stepped off to the side and talked quietly. Hudson's head flew up as, with a puzzled expression, he stared at Will and then at Patrick.

"Why, I had no notion there were boys, too," he said to Callahan. "We just heard of the girl needing a home."

"Well sir, when they was put aboard by that judge in Piqua," Callahan said. "It was plain they was together. The older boy, now he don't look much like the girl, but I believe the younger one does." He looked up in time to see his wife glance questioningly and he motioned her over.

As the adults stood apart talking, Tessa, Will and Patrick drew closer together. Emaline chattered at them, keeping up a steady, one-sided conversation.

"Oh, how I've always wanted to go on a long canal boat ride! How long did it take? Did you like it? I only ever been as far as Junction on a boat and that's only a couple of miles. I like it when we pass the 181-mile marker. I wish the boat would just stand still so's I could stay there long enough to think about it—181 miles to Cincinnati. I'd like to go there. Captain Callahan goes there all the time. He says it ain't, um, I mean, *isn't* much—just a city full of smoke and scoundrels . . ."

Tim Callahan spoke quietly to his wife and Mrs. Hudson. "Luke here says he don't know who the boys are. He and Eva just got word about the girl there."

Hudson scratched the back of his head. "I don't know that we have much room to spare . . ."

"Oh, how I wish they could stay with us, Eva," Martha said to Mrs. Hudson. "I'd like to think that if our own boys had lived . . ." Her voice trailed off. Emaline dashed up to her mother and begged to be allowed to show Tessa the little room they were to share in the brick house.

"Yes, yes, of course you may," Eva Hudson laughed. "But, Emaline, you are being rude to Mrs. Callahan."

"Oh, I'm ever so sorry, ma'am," the child said, looking down as twin blotches of color bloomed on her cheeks.

"That's quite all right," Martha Callahan replied. "Can I tell you a secret?"

Emaline turned her wide eyes on her mother. "May I hear it? Please?"

Her mother nodded. Smiling, Martha bent over and whispered loudly in the young girl's ear.

"I think that you and Tessa will be the best of friends," she said.

Martha Callahan had been right, Tessa thought. It hadn't taken long for the two girls to form a close bond, especially since Emaline gave everything her all, right down to her friendship. Although she was younger than Tessa, the child was smart and full of fun. They spent time swinging on the double swing that hung from one of the big oak trees in the yard. Luke had made it from a wide plank and some old towrope. The girls invented games and raced each other. Emaline's blond curls and pale skin made her look frail, but she ran faster than Tessa and could scamper up a tree, nimble as a squirrel.

Sometimes, although she felt much too old to be playing house, Tessa let Emaline serve her pretend tea. The younger girl, used to spending much of her time alone, had an active imagination. A wide oak stump in the yard was a table, two logs were the chairs. She had a small collection of chipped and cracked cups and saucers that she handled carefully as the finest china. Sticks, leaves, bird nests and acorns were often put to use to fill out the table.

The day after Tessa's arrival, Emaline must have decided that her new friend could be trusted. She suddenly stopped swinging and said. "Can you keep a secret?"

"Of course I can," Tessa said.

If you only knew, she thought.

"I have a secret hiding place just for my special things," Emaline said, jumping off the swing. "C'mon! I'll show you."

Making sure no one was watching, she ran to the corner of the house and counted five bricks up, then ten bricks across. Taking up a stick, she pried a brick out of the wall and set it on the ground. Tessa's mouth went dry as she watched Emaline take her playthings out of the wall. The hiding place she'd found in the wall of the lockkeeper's house was Emaline's! Tessa looked over the girl's shoulder, thinking perhaps the ring with the blue stone might be in the wall. When it wasn't, Tessa's hand went to her apron pocket, as if it might be there. But, it had disappeared along with her modern day clothes and the johnboat.

"See," Emaline said as she reached into the gap and brought out cracked teacups, a few chipped saucers and a couple of bent spoons. "Now we can play tea party!"

Tessa smiled down at the girl. She didn't know what she'd been expecting. Of course these things were treasure to Emaline, not gold and jewels.

"You know," Tessa said, picking up the brick and replacing it. "I was just thinking it's been a long time since I've been to a tea party."

Emaline happily gathered up her dishes and showed Tessa the tree stump she used for a table. Tessa showed Emaline how to make tiny fairy dishes from acorns and their knobby brown caps.

In the end it had been decided that Will and Patrick would stay with the Callahans on the *Dolley Madison* and now they spent their time traveling up and down the Miami and Erie Canal.

Tessa thought it must be fun living on a canal boat and thought of them each time a low, long boat with brightly painted shutters and doors approached.

The now familiar call of "Hey, lock," sounded through the early morning air, which meant the canal boat that approached was almost to Lock 32. Emaline stirred and opened her eyes.

"That's Captain Callahan's call!" She said and tried to sit up, but she was too tangled in her quilt cocoon.

Tessa laughed out loud as Emaline's head and feet, the only parts showing, wiggled in the dim early morning light.

"Don't just sit there laughing! Help me out of this! It's the *Dolley!*

"I might just leave you there," Tessa said with mock seriousness. "It'd teach you a lesson about stealing all the blankets."

"Please?" the younger girl begged. "I promise not to steal the bed coverings again." She managed to free an arm and made an "X" motion across the quilt. "Cross my heart! Now, get me loose!"

Tessa got up and acted like she was going downstairs.

"Please?" Emaline asked in a tiny voice. "Tessa?"

Without a word, Tessa turned around and pounced, and grabbing the edge of the top quilt, gave it a mighty yank. Emaline unwound and rolled onto the floor with a loud thump.

Hearing the giggles from the loft, Eva Hudson, who was stirring batter in a bowl, looked up at the ceiling. "You girls up there," she called. "I know you're awake. Best hurry now, the *Dolley's* coming and I want you to run out and invite the Callahans and the boys into breakfast. We're having johhnycakes. "

The sun was just throwing spears of golden light when the girls thundered down the steep plank stairs into the main room of the house. They used the game that Tessa had taught Emaline—rock, paper, scissors—to decide who won the privilege of being the first to use the little house out back.

"Scissors cuts paper! I get to go first," Emaline crowed and ran through the door.

When it was her turn, Tessa took her time walking down the worn dirt path. Every time she had to go to the bathroom, she longed for indoor plumbing. She also wished she wasn't expected to wear layer upon layers of clothing that had been packed in her trunk, especially in the middle of hot, humid summer. First came the thin, white cotton chemise and long, loose pants called "pantalets." Emaline referred to them as her "drawers" and "shimmy." Over top of these went a full slip, and at least one flounced petticoat, stiffened with starch. Both were to be drawn in at the waist and tied with a string. All the under things were trimmed with rows and rows of delicate handmade lace. Over the shimmy, drawers, and petticoats went a full dress that stood out like bell. The dress was then covered with an apron that Emaline called a "pinafore."

As Tessa washed her face and hands with a soft square of flannel, using water from the pitcher on the washstand by the back door, she couldn't help wondering if Will and Patrick had as much trouble as she did when it came time to dress or anything else. She was pretty sure she wouldn't get an answer, if she were to ask, at least not from Will, he wanted to be tough. Besides, Tessa imagined that Will loved being on the *Dolley Madison*. He always threw himself into his work, wanting to prove how mature he was. He was probably running barefoot and free like the other kids Tessa had seen on the boats passing through, while she was expected to wear tight, itchy clothes, stay out of the sun, folded hands in her lap, and "act like a little lady."

Chapter Ten

"He-ey, Lo-ock!" Tim Callahan called out as the *Dolley,* arrived at the lock.

A weak hooting sounded at the same time. Will turned and looked at the top deck and saw that Patrick was blowing on the captain's bugle. Patrick's face was red with the effort and his cheeks popped out like pink balloons, but the noise that came out reminded Will of a sick duck. It was nothing like the clear notes that the captain used to alert a locktender that his boat was approaching.

It had been almost three weeks since Will had helplessly watched Tessa, standing beside the lockkeeper's house, grow smaller and smaller. The days had passed quickly, but Will was still eager to see Tessa. He wondered how she was doing all alone. At least he had Patrick.

Will hoped that Tessa was enjoying living on the canal as much as he was, because he loved it. The life was hard, but it was never dull. Most of the people were rough, and often couldn't read or write. Whiskey flowed among the "canalers," and fights broke out over who got to go through locks first and or an insult about someone's boat. Although Will had only been on *"Miz Dolley,"* as the captain called his boat, for a short time, he was already a useful member of the crew. It was sort of weird, he thought. People didn't care what age you were back here. Kids weren't babied. They were expected to work and work hard, almost from the time they could walk. When a boy reached his age, he was doing a full day's work and then some. At first, Will thought he would die from the pain. After lifting crates, kegs and 50-pound sacks by the hour, every muscle in his body screamed. After several trips up and down the Miami and Erie and helping to load and unload his share of cargo—from ax handles to coal to barrels of vinegar and kegs of sorghum molasses—he was seasoned crew—a real bowsman. It hadn't taken long for him to toughen and now he could just about keep up with Adam.

It was only at night, in the moments right before he dropped off to a well-earned sleep that worry crept in. How did they get here? Would they ever get back? Did Mom and Dad know they were gone? He was supposed to keep an eye on Patrick. He did keep close watch over his little brother—not an easy job—but he couldn't help feeling like he was responsible for their trip through time. Maybe it was all just a dream.

"Will! Will!"

Will looked up. Emaline Hudson was on Lock 32, jumping up and down, up and down and waving her arms. Her bonnet bounced off and her fine, blond hair flew about, forming a halo about her head where it was touched by the early morning rays of the sun. Tessa stood quietly as Prudence and Mae pulled the *Dolley Madison* by its heavy towrope toward Lock 32.

Locking through was nothing to get excited about anymore, Will thought as the boat drew closer to the lock. He relaxed against a pile of floury-smelling wheat sacks. Full of grain, they were stacked higher than his head. Now when the towrope was tossed in Will's direction, he caught it and had it coiled before the shaggy-haired Brennan could work his chaw of tobacco around enough to spit. As for Patrick, he would have slept in the stalls with the mules if allowed. The "horses" that Patrick had admired so—Prudence and Mae and the relief team, Polly and Pearl— allowed him to pat their soft muzzles. In return, he brought bits of apple and carrot and insisted on helping Brennan brush them when it came time to bed the mules down for the night. Patrick often fell asleep at supper, his face dropping closer and closer to his plate as he dozed, so tired he was at the end of a day walking the towpath with the team. But, he always refused to come aboard and take a break when Martha asked if he wanted to "rest a spell." His face was even more freckled by the sun and his feet had grown tough as hide from the miles he walked barefoot beside Brennan the mule driver.

Adam, the tall, quiet young man Captain Callahan called "the boy-o," had shown Will the many jobs that needed to be done aboard the *Dolley Madison.* Tight brown curls escaped from under the cap the young man wore with the bill pulled low over his face. He spoke very little and taught Will by showing rather than telling. Once did he open up to Will. The *Dolley Madison* had just passed from the wide Maumee River into the guard lock at Independence, headed north for Toledo, or Port Lawrence, as some people called it. It had been about a week ago. The boat was riding low in the water, loaded with barrel staves cut from the thick woods of Paulding County. It was then that Adam spoke.

"Some says she's 250 miles long," he'd said.

"What?" Will asked, surprised to hear words from the young man.

"The Miami and Erie, some say she's near 250 miles long. In Cincinnati, they say it's more likely 284 miles, some say 301, if ya count some of the sidecuts."

"Oh," Will said, nodding, not sure what Adam was talking about.

"It only got to be called the Miami and Erie just here lately. It's really three canals." Adam said, and then was silent.

Will waited for him to finish his story as Adam, his cheeks bronzed by the hours he spent toiling under the summer sun, stared off across the countryside. When riding on a canal boat at around four miles an hour, Will thought, there was plenty of time to admire the landscape. Any faster and a captain risked being fined for speed. Going too fast caused waves that eroded the sides of the canal. Finally, curiosity won and he prodded Adam for more information.

"How can this be three canals in one?" he asked. "I've only seen one, except for the feeders that bring in the water."

"Well," Adam thought a moment, "she's only been complete— all the way from Cincy to Toledo—for about five years now. First section was the Miami Canal. It run from Cincinnati to Dayton. Opened way afore I was born—1825. Then the Miami Extension was added. Now, up here, about five years ago, we got the Wabash & Erie Canal coming in from Indiana. Now it's all one long canal from the Ohio River to Great Lake Erie. And some say it's 249 miles and some says it's 284. I'll tell you this much though," he said and then paused.

"What?" Will asked.

"I've lost count of how many times I've traveled any of 'em."

"Where are you from?" Will asked, eager to find out more about Adam Morgan. "You been on the canal all your life?"

"I spent most of my time on the canals," Adam said. "That I have."

But, further questions about his past or where he called home, went unanswered because Patrick ran up to the two older boys with the news that Martha had supper ready. Adam smiled, ruffling the boy's red hair with a sun-browned hand, and headed for the cornbread and molasses Martha had waiting.

Will forgot about his conversation with Adam when Patrick ran up from the back of the 77-foot-long boat.

"Hey! Will!" Patrick's cheeks bulged from a bite of apple. Two more were crammed in his pants pockets.

Spying the extra fruit, Will stared at Patrick.

"What?" Patrick asked around a mouthful of apple.

"Didn't you just have breakfast a little while ago? Are you going to eat all of those?" Will asked.

After a brief struggle with his pocket, Patrick finally tugged one of the other apples free and held up the slightly bruised fruit. "Martha gave 'em to me. You want one?" It came out sounding like "oo unt un?"

"No," Will said. "I just don't want to listen to you moaning and groaning all night with a stomachache."

Patrick swallowed noisily. "They aren't all for me," he said. "They're for Prudence and Mae. I already gave some to Polly and Pearl. They're going to switch in a little while. We always switch the teams at Lock 32," he added with the air of someone who had spent years instead of weeks on the canal.

They were traveling south. The *Dolley Madison* had floated out of the guard lock at Independence into the Maumee River, then back into the canal at Defiance and now was passing close by the bustling village of Charloe, on the Auglaize River. When he had first seen the many houses, stores and businesses, Will had been amazed. The Charloe he knew wasn't much more than a crossroads.

Will climbed the short ladder and ran lightly down the narrow catwalk that ran from the back cabin—the Callahan's tiny home—across the top of the mule stall to the front of the boat. He waved at Tessa as the boat drew closer to the lock. He hoped he'd get a chance to talk with Tessa alone. Maybe he could gently shove Emaline in his brother's direction to get rid of her for a while. Let Patrick be pestered for a change. Maybe Emaline could learn a few more things about bothering people from Patrick. He was a real pro.

The *Dolley Madison* hauled mainly cargo, but sometimes carried passengers. So far, all of them had found Patrick to be a delightful distraction during the long hours onboard. The problem was he talked too much. When he started to recount the events that had landed them on the Callahans' boat, Will did his best to get him onto another subject. Finally, scared that Patrick would get them into trouble, one day he pulled him aside.

"We're orphans," Will hissed under his breath to Patrick, after making sure they were alone. "When somebody asks you, you just say 'we're orphans.' And look sad. Then look down at your feet and shut up. I promise they won't ask any more questions."

"Okay, okay," Patrick said. "You don't have to yell at me."

"I'm *NOT YELLING* at you!"

Martha Callahan, who was hanging washing on a line strung between the rear cabin and the mules' stall, glanced in their direction with raised eyebrows.

Will lowered his voice. "I'm not *yelling* at you," he whispered to Patrick while grinning at Martha. "I'm just trying to get a very important point across to you. How are we going to explain to anyone that we just rode on in from the 21st Century in a rowboat? I can tell you this, I don't want to find out what they do to kids who they think are telling them big whoppers, do you?"

"Will," Patrick said, reaching up to pat his brother on the shoulder, "don't worry, we're just dreaming. Didn't you know that?"

"Well, this is the weirdest dream I've ever had." Will said as he turned and walked toward the cabin. He stopped and turned around. "What are you going to do when someone gets nosy?"

"Look sad. Say 'I'm an orphan.' Look at my feet. Shut up." Patrick repeated his orders.

"Good. Now, I have to go chop some kindling wood for Aunt Martha," Will said. "Stay out from underfoot." He headed for the cabin.

"Will?" Will stopped.

"What?"

"What's an orphan?"

"Hey-ey-ey Lo-ock!" Captain Callahan's voice suddenly boomed out again, bringing Will out of his thoughts.

The captain was putting on a show. The *Dolley Madison* didn't need to be announced because the entire Hudson family was waiting for her to float through the open upstream doors of Lock 32. The lock chamber was already full and the excess water from the canal flowed into the waste weir beside it. To prevent flooding, the weir took in the extra water when the lock gates were closed and directed it back into the canal below the lock. If another boat had just locked through, the *Dolley* would have had to wait while both the upstream and downstream gates were pushed closed, the small wicket doors cranked open, and the lock chamber allowed to fill.

"We get to go 'long! We get to go 'long to the Junction!" Emaline added singing to her bouncing. "You're to come to breakfast, then we're going to the Junction with you! Mama's making a carry-long lunch."

Tessa grabbed the younger girl's hand and pulled her out of the way as Emaline's father and the boat's crew, consisting of Adam and Will, secured the boat to the snubbing. Tying the boat up snuggly prevented the sides from bumping against the sides of the lock. Patrick scrambled over the side and hurried over to assist Brennan on the towpath by helping unhitch Polly and Pearl.

Tessa walked over to Will just as he was brushing his hands off on his tattered overalls. For the moment she was alone, since Emaline was admiring Patrick as he rubbed Mae's legs down with a handful of clean straw.

Will sat on an overturned keg and pulled another up for Tessa.

Tessa looked at him and a big smile crossed her face. "How's Patrick? Is he okay? You are a mess," she said. "Look at you. Ripped up ol' overalls, no shoes. You need a haircut. But, boy, am I glad to see you, dirt and all!"

"Thanks a lot and I'm happy to see you, too," he said, grinning back. "You know Patrick. He's just fine. Hey, when you work, you get dirty."

"I bet you could plant potatoes in that ring around your neck," Tessa said. "Hey, speaking of rings," she lowered her voice to a whisper, "I can't find that ring anywhere. It was in the pocket of my shorts and," she said, as she looked down at her dress, "well, of course they disappeared, but the ring went with them, wherever that is."

"Who knows?" Will said. "I've given up trying to figure things out. Besides, I've been too busy working."

"I work!" Tess snapped. "I work all the time. Weeding the garden, picking bugs off the plants by hand, churning butter, whacking dirt out of rugs, feeding the chickens. Just look at my hands," she said, turning her hands palms up. "They're covered with blisters. And they don't have any real medicine around here. Do you know what they use? Goose fat! Stinky goose grease is supposed to cure everything! I've got a blister on my heel right now from these boots, but I am not about to go telling anyone about it. Aunt Eva would like nothing better than another excuse to open up that crock of slime and slap some more of it on me."

Will looked down at her feet, encased in tightly fitting ankle-high black boots. Wiggling his own toes in the cool dust, he felt sorry for her.

"So why are you wearing boots? Most of the kids I see are barefoot."

"Didn't you hear Emaline? We're going on the boat with you to Junction. I guess it's supposed to be a really big deal. Then Uncle Luke is supposed to bring the wagon. I guess to haul stuff back here. And you all go on your merry way." Tessa swiped at a trickle of sweat that ran down the side of her face. "It's so hot. You wouldn't believe how many layers of clothes I have on under this thing." She flapped her apron at her face, then pushed the long sleeves of her dress up her forearms as far as their snug-fitting cuffs would allow.

"Yeah," Will replied, "what I wouldn't give for can of pop right now."

"Oh, yeah," Tessa sighed, "one that's been packed in ice."

"I can't imagine what we're going to do in Junction all day. There's nothing there but a few houses and a couple of churches," Tess said. "And we have a whole five cents to spend."

"Don't be so sure," Will said. "Have you been to Charloe?"

"Well, not since we, well, you know—got here. Why?"

"It's not a thing like it is now . . . um, we remember it," Will said. "Houses everywhere, stores and shops and roads. There's a blacksmith, even a courthouse and a hotel —it's like a regular town!"

"This is the freakiest, isn't it? Tess asked.

"Yeah, I wonder when I'm going to wake up," he said.

"Can two people be having the same dream at the same time?"

"You mean three people," Will said.

"Three?"

Will jabbed a thumb in Patrick's direction. "He's says we're just dreaming."

"Well, are we? Pinch me." Tess thrust her arm at Will, bravely turned her head away and covered her eyes with the other hand. Will did nothing.

When the pinch didn't happen, she exclaimed happily. "I knew it! I knew it! I am asleep! It is a dream! I didn't feel a thing."

"You dork, I'm not going to pinch you!" Will said, shoving her arm away.

Tessa looked puzzled.

"Look, I already tried it." He showed her several small, round bruises on his own arm. "Take my word for it. You can feel the pinch. It hurts."

"Don't let Aunt Eva see those," Tess warned, seeing his arm. "Goose grease."

The two sank into thoughtful silence. After a moment Tessa said, "I bet our moms are worried sick about us."

"Yeah," Will agreed. "What do you think we should do? We can't stay here forever," he said, scratching in the dust with his big toe.

"I don't know," Tessa said.

"Neither do I," Will said.

"I wonder what our dads would do if this happened to them," Tessa said.

"Our dads would love this," Will laughed a little.

"Yeah, I can tell *you* do."

"You know," Will said, "actually, I really do like living on a canal boat. The Callahans are great. They treat me like . . . like . . . like what I do really matters. I even get paid."

"You get an allowance at home, don't you?" Tessa asked.

"Yeah, but that's for taking out the trash and making my bed. This is different," Will said. "I mean, I do the same work as everyone else. No one ever says I can't because I'm just a kid. And you know what's really weird? I don't miss TV or the computer or even video games."

"I sure wish I could work on the boat. It looks like a lot more fun that staying here and being a *proper lady*. I'm sure it's better than tea parties and sewing and stuff." Tessa said, scratching her knee through a thick stocking.

"Well, it's not all fun," Will said. "It just about wears me out trying to keep an eye on Patrick all the time. He is going to blow it and tell somebody about us. I just know it. At least you don't have to worry about that."

"That Emaline is no angel," Tessa said.

"BLA-A-A-AT!"

Tessa shrieked in surprise. Will leaped completely off his seat and then sat down hard, his behind smacking the ground as the captain's bugle blasted in their ears.

"Patrick! Gosh darn it!" Will spun around intending to grab the horn from his brother, only to find it clutched tightly in Emaline's hand. The girl grinned at Will, giggled, gave him a shove, then turned and ran. Patrick was right behind her.

Tess, still seated on her keg, folded her arms and smiled dryly down at Will. "See what I mean? C'mon, let's go get breakfast. We're having johnnycakes, whatever that is."

"Oh, we've had those," Will said. "They're pretty much like pancakes, only made with cornmeal. Kind of dry, but I'll eat just about anything anymore."

Chapter Eleven

The *Dolley Madison* slowly drew closer to the lock. Tessa grabbed Emaline's hand and yanked her out of the way as Adam and Will secured the boat to the snubbing post beside the lock. Tying the boat up prevented its sides, just inches from the inside walls of the lock, from being damaged when the water level was raised and lowered. Today the *Dolley* was riding high on the water since she carried only a small amount of cargo and she responded to the slightest tug on the towrope.

Before the boat entered the chamber, Patrick scrambled down the gangplank and hurried over to help Brennan, who was on the towpath unhitching Polly and Pearl.

Tessa walked over to Will just as he was brushing his hands off on his tattered overalls. For the moment she was alone, since Emaline was Patrick's adoring helper. She watched intently as the boy rubbed Mae's legs down with clean straw. She stood eagerly at attention, a bunch of straw clenched in each small hand. Martha had already left the boat and joined Aunt Eva in the kitchen. The good-natured shouts of Captain Callahan, Brennan and Uncle Luke filled the bright morning air as they pushed the great balance beams that opened and closed the lock gates.

The trip to Junction on the *Dolley Madison* was one she had taken many times before, but never on the canal. Tessa was amazed at how deep and dark the woods were. The familiar roads and farms would be years in the future.

"What's that stone thing over there?" Tessa asked Will as the *Dolley Madison*, now pulled by Polly and Pearl, drew closer to the bustling village. She pointed to a stone post beside the towpath.

"Oh, that's a mile marker. Um . . . let's see," Will leaned out over the water to get a better look. "Looks like it says 181."

"That's the 181-mile marker," Emaline chimed in as she joined Tessa and Will at the rail. "From this very spot to Cincinnati is exactly 181 miles. I'd like to travel 181 miles some day. That's ever so long a journey, but Mother says that someday we'll go. She says that there's so much to see and do there. It's a real city. Father says they call it the Queen City and that it has seven hills, just like ancient Rome. That's in Italy," she turned and explained to Patrick.

"I knew that," Patrick replied defensively.

"I wish I could travel on the *Dolley Madison* with you and Patrick all the way to Cincinnati," Emaline said wistfully, turning back to Will and Tessa. "Wouldn't we have ever so much fun, Tessa? Have you ever been to the Queen City?"

"Well . . . I . . ." Tessa glanced at Will and saw that he was shaking his head "no."

"I guess I always wanted to go to Cincinnati . . ." She trailed off, but Emaline was already chattering on about how excited she was to get to Junction and spend her pennies, for to her amazement, her father had given the girls not one, but five coins each.

"I know I'll get candy," she was saying. "I always get candy. Don't you always, Patrick?"

"Always what?" Patrick said. He was leaned over the side of the boat, tossing pebbles from the collection in his pocket into the water.

"Always buy *candy*," Emaline repeated. She looked down at her bonnet ribbons and discovered they were in a knot. "I think I like peppermint sticks the very best," she said, working away at loosening the snarl. She stopped messing with the tangled bonnet strings for a moment and staring at them said, "Then there's ribbon candy. I like that, too."

"Sure, I like candy," Patrick said. "I like Snickers and M&M's and . . ."

Will grabbed his brother with both hands and hauled him back until both feet landed on the deck with a thump.

"Hey!" Patrick yelped as Will, with his bare foot, gave him a firm nudge on the seat of his overalls.

Patrick clutched his rear and whirled to glare at Will. "What ya do that for?"

Will, checking to make sure Emaline's attention was still on her knotted ribbons, put a thumb and index finger to the corner of his mouth and made a twisting motion, as if turning a key.

Patrick nodded his head to show that he understood, and then spoke to Emaline. "Yeah, peppermint sticks." He glanced back at his brother. "Definitely, positively peppermint sticks. My favorite. My very, very best favorite. Peppermint sticks." He made big circles on his belly. "M-m-m-m, yum-mee. . . . pep . . ."

Will glared at him.

"What?" Patrick said innocently.

The children rode along in silence, enjoying the passing scenery. A muskrat swam smoothly ahead of the boat, making a V-shaped wake in the water.

"Uh-oh," Will remarked when he saw the little animal dive under the water.

"What?" Tessa asked.

"That muskrat is up to no good," Will said.

"That little thing?" Tessa said. "What harm could he possibly do?"

"Muskrats and groundhogs, even fox, burrow into the berm and weaken them," Will said.

"The berm? You mean the sides of the canal?" Tessa asked.

"Yeah," Will said. With the air of an expert, he launched into an explanation about the danger muskrats posed to the canal. "Even though the berm is 36 feet wide at the base, after animals dig enough tunnels, there can be cave-ins. And if there's a lot of rain, the berm gets soggy and whole sections collapse, towpath and all. Then the canal breaches."

"Breaches?"

"Washes out, breaks down," Will said. "And Adam says the farmers who own the land that floods sure don't like it one bit."

"Seems hard to believe a cute little animal like that could cause all that trouble," Tessa said. "Poor things."

"Poor things!" Will exclaimed.

After the mile marker the boat passed over a stone culvert, built for the purpose of carrying the canal and towpath over a creek. They had floated over an aqueduct not far from Lock 32, where the canal crossed over wide Flat Rock Creek, but Tessa heard Captain Tim call it Crooked Creek.

Wow, Tessa thought as they approached the town of Junction. The Junction that Tessa had known all her life consisted of a few homes, a bunch of little old houses, abandoned and vine-covered, plus a couple of churches—nothing like this bustling town of streets and alleys. Several canal boats were waiting at a wharf to load cargo. Horse-drawn wagons, some full, some empty, trundled to and away from the canal. Wood smoke and the loud metallic clanging of a blacksmith's hammer filled the air. A mob of barefoot children and barking dogs ran noisily past, sending a hen squawking into the path of a passing horse. It neighed and reared back, nearly unseating the rider while the chicken scuttled off, unharmed.

"Wow!" This time Tessa spoke aloud.

"I know," Will said. "It's really something, isn't it? Captain Tim said Junction's got lots of stores and hotels and stuff. And saloons. Stay away from them. Some of those guys are pretty rough."

"Oh, yeah, sure, that's the first place I'll be sure to go—a saloon. Have you been been up this far yet?" Tessa asked.

"Yes, and we've been south of here, down by Dayton and Cincinnati," Will said. "Toledo's different, too, though. Captain Tim said it used to be two towns—Vistula and Port Lawrence. He said that the way Junction is growing, it won't be long until it's bigger than either Fort Wayne or Toledo."

"Junction . . . bigger than Toledo? I can hardly believe it." Tessa said.

"When . . . or if . . . we ever do get back home, nobody is going to believe any of this," Will said.

Tessa peered closely at her cousin. "You aren't in a big hurry to get back, are you?"

Will looked down at his dust-covered bare feet, the tips of his ears glowing, the muscle in his jaw working. "Well . . ." He looked up. "No. I'm not. Not that it matters, because I wouldn't know how even if I wanted to."

The sun was high, small and white hot by the time everyone gathered under the shade of a towering oak to share the "carry-long dinner." Compared to the picnic food that Will was used to, it was plain fare. It didn't include the potato chips and hot dogs he was used to, but Eva's fried chicken and corn bread with fresh honey tasted even better. Will hungrily helped himself to several pieces of each plus some of Martha's baked beans, kept warm all morning, wrapped in an old quilt.

"Ah," Captain Tim leaned back against the wide expanse of the oak tree's trunk and rubbed his belly. "Thank you, ladies."

Martha turned to Eva. "I must say that honey is some of the best I've ever had."

"Oh, that's some the bee man brought by a while back. Said he found a bee tree in a stand of locust trees. It is good honey, though. Very light."

Will let the conversation wash around him as he scootched to the opposite side of the tree, and like the captain, lay back against its wide trunk. He tipped his straw hat over his face to block out the bright patches of sun that worked through the canopy of leaves. It felt good to do nothing. Folding his arms behind his head, he sighed and let his thoughts wander back over the past few weeks.

At first the muscles in his shoulders and legs ached from loading and unloading cargo—stacks of wood, crates, boxes, kegs and barrels, bags of grain. The thick towrope was rough and rubbed his hands until they were raw and blistered. He'd worked through it and they had quickly grown smooth and tough as tanned leather. Being a canaler meant long days and short nights, especially in the summer, especially on the nights when the moon spilled its light down and turned the canal into a river of silver. After a very short rest, the crew was up and going again before dawn.

Although crusty old Brennan was the hoggee, or muleskinner, on the *Dolley,* Will had noticed kids as young as Patrick walking beside the mules on the towpaths and sometimes riding on the back of one of the sturdy animals. Patrick had seen them too, and Will could almost hear the gears grinding in his brother's head as he tried to figure out a way to convince the Callahans that he, too, had what it took to be a real muleskinner.

"Hey! Will!" He heard his name called from far away and gradually became aware of heavy breathing. He slowly opened his eyes. He was eyeball to eyeball with Patrick, who had removed the hat from Will's face and was holding it high in the air, out of his brother's reach.

"Huh!" Will shot upright and looked around wild-eyed.

Emaline hovered over the boy's shoulder. "Will! Wake up!"

"I'm awake," Will said sleepily as he ran his hands over his face. He made an unsuccessful grab for his hat. "I'm awake, I said."

Tessa laughed as Will tried again and snatched his hat back from his brother.

"What are you laughing at?" He snarled at Tessa as he jammed the hat back on his head.

"You."

"I wasn't asleep."

"Yes, you were, unless you snore when you're awake."

"I wasn't asleep and I don't snore!"

"Oh, okay, you don't snore," Tessa said, rolling her eyes at Emaline, who giggled.

"Well, anyway, we're allowed to go look around. Then we're to meet at the boat. The Callahans want to leave this afternoon and Uncle Luke needs to get back to the lock," Tessa said, turning back toward the bustling village.

"Okay. Yeah, I guess that's okay. I've got some money . . . that I *earned*," he added proudly.

Will, Tessa, and Patrick, led by Emaline, headed toward the stores that lined the dusty street. Emaline vowed she knew where the best place for getting the most candy for the smallest outlay of coin. Eva and Martha began packing up the remains of the noon meal into baskets and planned to follow shortly.

Emaline pointed out her favorite store, but the children had trouble getting to the door because of a crowd that had gathered in the middle of the road. Two men were in the middle, one waving a large piece of paper with bold printing on it. A shotgun rested in the crook of his elbow. His partner, who was taller and had a thick, black beard, shouted to the crowd.

" . . . an' they's a reward o' forty dollah . . ." he said, turning slowly around, his inky eyes glittering.

At this news, the group of men made up of farmers, canalers and mill workers, muttered and murmured.

"A hunert and fifty dollars!"

"By criminy, that's a lot o' money!"

"I ain't seen that much money in all my days," another voice said.

"Stay here," Will ordered Patrick and Emaline. "I want a better look. C'mon, Tess."

Tessa hesitated as she looked first at the two younger children then back at Will, who had already wormed his way into the crowd. "I'll be right back," she told Emaline. "Wait here with Patrick. Don't move." Then she followed Will as he pushed through the jostling onlookers.

Will, with Tessa clutching his shirt to keep from being separated in the crowd, squeezed between a couple of canalers and emerged into the center of the circle. The heat and the smell of sweat was so strong that he held his breath. Having broken through the press of bodies, he was close enough to see the words on the poster, but couldn't read them because the man with the paper was waving it around so that the print blurred into black blobs.

"Will!" Tessa pulled on his arm. "We have to get back. We can't leave those kids alone." She turned around and squeezed her way back to where the younger children were waiting impatiently. Will followed reluctantly.

Chapter Twelve

Once inside the general store, like bees to a flower, Patrick and Emaline headed straight for a long counter lined with a selection of candies displayed in stout jars. On tiptoe, they pored over fat little peppermint puffs, sparkling crystals of rock candy, rich and glossy molasses taffy, shiny black licorice strings, satiny striped ribbon candy and red and white peppermint sticks.

Will watched the children, but his mind was still on the crowd outside.

"I wonder what they did that was so awful people would pay money to catch them," he said quietly to Tessa.

"I don't know," she said. "Maybe they murdered somebody or stole something valuable."

"They're runaways," the man behind the counter said.

Will whipped around. He didn't know he had spoken loudly enough to be overheard.

"Running away from what?"

"They're slaves, boy."

"Slaves!"

"I thought Ohio was a free state," Tessa said, stepping closer to the storekeeper. "There have never been any slaves in Ohio. We studied it in school."

"Where you been, girl? The papers have been full of it. Haven't you heard of the Fugitive Slave Law?" He leaned over and pulled out a paper identical to the one the man outside had been waving around. "Here. Read it."

Will stepped up and took the poster. Tessa peered over his shoulder.

$150 REWARD!
Ran away the 28th of June, Negro man, Tom, he calls himself—
THOMAS BROWN.
Aged about forty to fifty years of age.
He is dark of complexion, with a scar running
from his left eye to his chin.
He is about five feet ten or eleven inches high.

At the same time his wife, **SUSAN BROWN,** *eloped with him.*
She is aged about thirty-five years. She is of small stature,
about five feet high, her teeth are much decayed.
The above reward will be paid for the negroes if delivered
to me or secured in any jail so that I may get them.

Zachariah Berry, *of Cumberland County, Tennessee.*

REWARD!

When he finished reading, Will felt sick. He hastily handed the announcement back to the storekeeper.

"You keep it. I don't need it. There'll be enough of these plastered around town," the storekeeper said.

"Uh, thanks," Will said uncertainly. He quickly folded the paper and stuffed it into his back pocket. "What's the Fugitive Slave Law?" he asked.

"The Slave Act? Why, it's Congress' way of making trouble for poor souls who don't need any more than the heap they already got, that's what it is," The man mopped at his forehead with a corner of his apron. "It means helping any slave, who manages to get away, can land you in jail, too. And a lot poorer, to boot, by the time you pay the fines."

"Then even though Ohio's supposed to be a free state, it's still not very safe, is it?" Tess asked.

"No, missy, it ain't. And them slave catchers out there ain't exactly the finest citizens, and they ain't come to town for a play party. We don't need their kind around here. We already have enough problems coming from the saloons and such. They'll just get everybody stirred up over that big cash reward."

Will wandered about the cramped, dusty dry goods store. He hoped to find a pencil with good, dark lead and some drawing paper, so he could draw the *Dolley Madison* and some of the other interesting sights along the canal, but he couldn't put the slave catchers out of his mind. The afternoon heat made it hard to breathe in the close air of the little shop. Flies buzzed lazily from spot to spot, clinging to everything and leaving behind sticky brown spots. Will brushed one away as it droned in his face.

"Hey, Will. Tess," Patrick called. "C'mere. Lookit the candy. What kind are you gonna get?"

Will and Tess joined him at the candy counter.

"Well, what may I get for you, young lady?" the storekeeper asked. "Wait, I think I know. A fine peppermint stick, perhaps?" he asked as he withdrew a sample from its jar with a flourish.

Will wanted to laugh at the way Tess wrinkled up her nose when she saw the fly-specks dotting the surface of the jar.

"Uh, no. No, thank you," she said hastily.

The storekeeper, disappointed with her reply, turned toward Will. "How about you then, young man?" He held the stick up to his nose and sniffed. "Ah, peppermint. Cooling on a hot day like today, eh?"

Will shook his head. "No, thanks. But, I would like this pencil and I need some paper."

"We-e-ell," the storekeeper said, quickly tossing the candy stick back into its jar. Rubbing the palms of his hands on his apron, he said, "A young man with a little coin to jingle in his pocket." He leaned over the jars, peering at Will. "Say, I don't recall seeing you around Junction. Just move in? Or just passin' through?"

"I've been through Junction before, just never came in here until now," Will said.

"We're on the *Dolley Madison!*" Patrick chipped in.

"I know the Callahans," the shopkeeper said. "I don't recall that they was blessed with younguns."

"Well, sir!" Patrick said happily. "They are now! Now, they've got us . . ." he looked up at his brother, grinned, and winked knowingly, " . . . *orphans.*"

The man's face lit up at the prospect of some news. Fear zinged through Will and he quickly nudged Patrick aside. The shopkeeper's curiosity about the Callahans' *orphans* could be dangerous.

"Hey!" Patrick said, elbowing his way back up to the counter. He looked at his brother, puzzled. "I said we was orphans, didn't I, Will?"

Will put his hands on Patrick's shoulders, wheeled him around and pushed him toward Tess, nodding in the direction of the door. The man behind the counter was watching with a great deal of interest.

"Paper, I need paper . . ." Will reminded the shopkeeper, his voice cracking nervously.

"Hey! Wait a minute! I want to pick out my own candy!" Patrick protested loudly.

A couple of other customers looked up at the disturbance. Tess swooped over, dragging Emaline by the wrist.

"Get them outta here," Will said to Tess out of the corner of his mouth.

"But, Will . . ." Patrick protested, "I wanted some . . ." His words were muffled as Tess wrapped her arm around her younger cousin, and with Emaline still in tow, wrestled both children toward the door.

"And . . . and . . . candy! I want lots of candy." Will hastily added. "Two of each. I'm buying."

Tessa hurried the two children along. "Will's getting it, don't you worry. Let's go outside. It's just too hot in here."

Relief washed over Will as Tess hustled the puzzled children out of the store.

"Well, well, well!" The man behind the counter rubbed his hands together, the news of orphans chased away by the chance for a sizable sale. He started opening jars. "A large amount of coin to jingle."

Chapter Thirteen

"Thank you ever so much for the candy, Will," Emaline said. Her cheeks bulged as she pushed another four inches of licorice into her mouth. In her other hand was a brown paper wrapped package tied with a thin string. She slipped her finger under the bow and hefted the bundle. "It's candy enough to last till Christmas!"

"So much for those extra coins jingling in my pocket that guy was so excited about," Will said to Tess. "That candy wiped me out. Now I'm broke. I barely had enough to pay for a pencil and some paper. That's the only reason I went in there in the first place."

Tess punched him lightly on the upper arm. "Oh, you're just an old softy under that hard crust."

"No, I'm not," Will said. "I had to do something to get that guy's big nose sniffing in another direction. He was starting to bug me."

"He was just trying to be friendly."

"That kind of friendliness could get us into big trouble. You're almost as bad as Patrick," Will muttered. "What if someone figures out where we really came from?"

"They would laugh and think we were just telling stories," Tessa said. "Whew! It's hot out here! Let's find some shade."

Will, Tessa, Patrick and Emaline stood for a moment in front of the store, getting used to the glare outside after the dimness inside. It was a busy day in Junction. Acrid smoke hung in the air mixed with billows of tan dust as wagons rumbled back and forth from the canal. Men shouted at mules and horses and each other while the rhythmic clang of a blacksmith's hammer rang out. Keeping off to the side, the group turned toward the canal, following a wagon loaded with barrel staves cut from the deep woods surrounding the village.

"Hey, Emaline, look!" Patrick said, tucking two candy canes up under his lip. "I'm a walrus." He turned around, and walking backwards, flapped his arms stiffly while making barking noises.

"Walruses don't bark, seals bark," Will said.

"Yuh-hunh, walruses do too make a noise just like that," Patrick said around his peppermint tusks. "I saw it on the Zoo Channel."

Tessa shot a look of alarm at Will, who was looking down at the paper he had just purchased. Patrick's talk of television, an invention that would not be found in the average American household until well into the 1950's, caused Will's head to snap up and he stopped dead in his tracks.

Patrick, realizing his blunder, also halted and clapped both hands to his mouth. "Oops," he said in a small voice, his eyes wide as they rolled in Will's direction.

Emaline, busy chewing, continued on. Her jaw still working on the licorice, she dug into her sack of candy, so completely absorbed in choosing another piece that she didn't hear Patrick's comment.

"This candy makes me thirsty," she said around the mouthful of sweet stuff. "I want to get a drink. C'mon, there's a well around the corner."

Emaline finished drinking deeply from the tin cup that dangled by the piece of twine that attached it to the low well by the roadside. She turned to hand the cup to Tessa. Thirsty from their dusty walk, Tessa was reaching for the mug, when suddenly, two riders on horseback thundered around the corner, headed straight for Emaline.

Will reached for her, but Tessa was closer. The mug of water went flying as Tessa leaped, and grabbing the child's pinafore, yanked her out of the path of the trampling hooves. The force threw both girls to the ground and they tumbled over and over. The back of Emaline's head knocked into Tessa's face and pain exploded in her mouth and nose. They finally rolled to a stop in a jumble of arms and legs. The riders glanced back in the children's direction, then jabbed boot heels into their horses' sides and galloped off. Emaline's package lay trampled in the road and licorice whips, peppermint sticks and rock candy were scattered in the dirt.

Tessa scrambled to her hands and knees. A trickle of red ran out of one nostril and over her top lip, while her bottom lip was already puffed to twice its normal size. Sobbing, she crawled toward Emaline in what felt like slow motion.

A crowd gathered instantly and Will had to push his way through to get to the girls. Tessa knelt over Emaline, who lay very still. Her bonnet was thrown to the side and her fine hair was caked with dirt. Crimson drops, running from a long gash on her forehead, were bright against her white skin.

"Emaline!" Tessa cried. She looked up. "Will! Do something!"

Eva Hudson ran up, and falling to the ground, pulled her daughter' limp body into her lap. "Emaline!" She shook the child gently. Emaline's eyes were closed, but she stirred slightly.

The crowd parted, making way for Luke Hudson as he dashed up, boots pounding on the hard baked earth. In one smooth movement, he scooped his daughter from Eva's lap, and carefully cradling her in his strong arms, ran back up the street in the direction the children had just come. Will was helping Tessa to her feet when Martha Callahan breathlessly arrived. Tessa was wobbly but able to walk with Martha on one side and Will on the other as they followed the Hudsons.

Luke, with Eva close behind, ran until he reached a neatly painted clapboard house. He kicked open the door, shouting, "Doc! Doctor Ayres!"

"Thank God," Eva breathed when Emaline's eyes fluttered open.

"Well, young lady," Dr. Ayres said as he closely examined the bump on her head. "You gave everyone a good fright back there!" Turning to Luke Hudson, he said, "What happened?"

"I'm not sure," Luke replied. "I think she may have been trampled by a horse."

"That's not it, exactly," a voice said from the doorway. It was Will. "Tess *saved* Emaline from being trampled."

"Tessa!" Eva exclaimed. "Where is she?"

"She's out here on the porch," Martha said, appearing behind Will. "I think she'll be all right, but she's in need of aid."

Later, back on the *Dolley Madison,* Tessa pressed a cloth to her face, but it no longer brought any relief to her throbbing lip. Cool when first applied, it had quickly grown hot, and now it was hard to tell it apart from the humid evening air. She leaned against Will's shoulder and fought back tears that pushed against her closed lids. The taste of blood was still thick and metallic on her tongue. And the pain where Emaline's head had smacked into her mouth, spread up and out like the branches on a tree, making her entire head ache and thump with every beat of her heart.

They were heading back to the little brick house at Lock 32. Tessa and Will sat on the deck, their backs pressed against the mule stable. Tim Callahan was at the rudder. Walking beside one of the mule teams on the towpath, swinging a lantern, Brennan led the way. Tessa could hear him talking to the mules, encouraging them in his rough voice. Although an occasional gruff curse was thrown in, Tessa knew Brennan was really soft-hearted for she had often heard him crooning Irish lullabies to the long-eared animals and feeding them a handful of oats out of the ample store in his pockets.

"At least it didn't knock any of your teeth out." Will's voice, filled with fake cheer, came through the pounding in Tessa's head.

"M-m, hm," was all she could manage.

"I'm sorry, Tess," he said. "I didn't mean to make you talk."

"S'okay," she whispered, and winced at the pain caused by moving her lips.

"I should have been watching out for her," Will said in a low voice. "She could have been killed. *You* could have been killed."

In the west, a lick of lightning slithered across the sky, followed by a low rumble. Dark clouds were boiling up and blocking out the angry red sunset.

"It's all my fault," a tiny voice came out of the gloom. "Me and my big mouth, showing off and talking about the Animal Channel."

"Patrick," Will said softly. "It was not your fault. How can you think that?"

The only response was a snuffle.

Being careful not to jar Tessa, Will got up, went to his brother and gathered the boy onto his lap. Patrick turned his face into Will's thin shoulder and sobbed.

Tessa, already close to tears, couldn't stop them from rolling, hot and stinging into the cut on her lip. She could hear Patrick's muffled sobs and the soft thump of Will's hand, as he patted his brother's back.

"It's okay. It's okay." Will said over and over.

"I want to go home, Will," Patrick said.

Another needle of lightening stitched through the blackness and a cool gust of wind pushed up the canal and ruffled the hair on their sweaty foreheads.

"Will . . ." Tessa whispered. "I want to go home, too."

"I know, I know," Will said. "I do, too. But, how do we get there?"

"It's a miracle she wasn't killed," Martha Callahan said, wringing a piece of flannel into a basin of water. "I'm just going to run this fresh cloth out to poor Tessa. I'll be back directly."

Luke and Eva Hudson leaned over the built-in bed in the Callahans' tiny cabin on the *Dolley Madison*. Emaline, very small in the middle of the fat feather tick, lay with her head wrapped in a clean, white bandage. Her eyes were open and the sparkle in her blue eyes, while dimmed slightly by a headache, had returned.

"I'm . . . I'm . . . *okay,*" she said, trying out one of Patrick's favorite words. "My head just hurts a little. Just a tiny little bit. Where is Tessa? And Patrick and Will?" She asked as she flung the coverlet off and tried to climb out of bed.

"Whoa! Whoa! Hold your horses, there young lady," Luke put his hand on his daughter's shoulder and gently pushed her back down. "You've taken quite a tumble."

"The doctor says you're to rest until he comes out to check on you tomorrow," Eva added.

Emaline's head fell back onto the pillow. "That's forever and ever! I feel fine. Really, I do. Even Doctor Ayres said I just fainted. I wasn't really uncon . . . unconch . . . unconstitutional."

"I believe you mean unconscious," her mother said, smiling. "Even so, you had best follow doctor's orders."

"And anyways, I wasn't!" Her head hurt a little more than she wanted to admit, so Emaline didn't offer any more argument. She plucked peevishly at the blanket. "Do I have to keep this on? It's so hot! Can I have a drink of water?"

Martha had returned. "What do you think, Martha?" Eva asked. "Do you think she could have it off?"

Martha dabbed at the perspiration on her own face with the back of her hand. "Land knows it is hot. It's about to blow up a storm." She poured a mug of water from a pitcher and carried it over the Emaline, who drank thirstily. "In the meantime, as long as she's not chilled, I reckon it would be safe to let the child decide for herself if she needs covered up or not."

A thunderclap rang like a gunshot and a drop of rain hit Tessa's forehead, pinprick sharp and icy cold. She got up, and holding the cloth against her throbbing lip, ran for the cabin. At Aunt Eva and Martha's insistence, she climbed into the big bed and settled in beside Emaline. As she sank into the heavenly softness, Tessa thought lying on a goose down filled mattress must be like sleeping on a cloud. At first it was hot and stuffy, but as the wind blew away the heat outside, cooler air began to seep into the little house. Tessa's muscles were sore as the day after the first softball practice in spring. The rain sounded like hundreds of little fingers tapping on the cabin roof, but it was a sleepy sound. The *Dolley Madison* rocked slightly in the wind.

When Tessa heard Martha and Eva preparing supper in the boat's tiny kitchen, or galley, as the Captain called it, her thoughts turned to her mother at the stove in the kitchen on the farm. Longing for home and all that was safe and familiar washed over her. She closed her eyes and willed herself to sleep. Maybe when she woke she would be in her own bed, with Margie and Erie curled snug at her feet. Tessa dozed off as the thumping of the mules in their stalls, the smell of supper sizzling in a skillet, the low rumble of the men's voices and the thunder all twisted and turned and tangled with each other and the steady sound of falling rain.

Emaline sat up, carefully holding her bandaged head, and took note of Tessa's puffy mouth and swollen nose. "Mother? Isn't there anything we can do for Tess?"

"Yes, there is," Eva replied softly, putting her finger to her lips. "We can let her rest."

Chapter Fourteen

Luke went out, climbed to the roof of the cabin and joined Tim, who leaned easily against the tiller in spite of the rain. The captain had planned to continue north from Junction that afternoon, but had offered to bring the injured girls back in the *Dolley Madison*. It was a much smoother trip back to Lock 32 on the canal than jolting over rough roads in a wagon.

"How are the girls?" The captain asked.

"Both asleep," Luke said. "You know how children are, they'll be up and around in no time at all."

A gust of wind pushed the *Dolley Madison* toward the side of the canal, and with a slight movement of the rudder, the captain brought the boat back on course. He nodded to the towering clouds. "We're about to get our dust settled real good, Luke. Don't think we're goin' to make it back before it hits. I'd have had Brennan put on another mule to speed things up, but at this point, the extra speed would have saved us about the same amount of time it would take to stop and hitch 'er up."

"We need this rain," Luke said. "Any idea who those characters were that almost ran down the girls?"

Callahan turned and squinted into the weather. "I don't know them by name, mind you. But, they sure didn't make it a secret what their business was, plastering them flyers all over town." He leaned over and spat into the choppy water. "There's few things in this world would cause growed men to run down youngun's in their path . . . and the thing that come first to my mind is money."

"Money?"

"Yessir. Money—and not just a little bit of it. Those fellers are after more than loose change. There's a sizeable amount of hard

85

cash to be found in returning escaped slaves to their owners—
and they aim to get it, with no heed to how much human sufferin'
and misery they cause."

Just then a shout from behind caused the men to look back in
the direction of Junction. Someone was trying to catch up with
the *Dolley Madison*. A black shadow, lit by an occasional flash of
lightening, was running down the towpath.

Patrick made his way toward the captain. "Look!" he said,
pointing to the towpath.

The captain peered through the slanting rain at the figure,
then barked "Brennan! Hold up!"

Brennan stopped the mules and the boat's forward motion
gradually slowed. Large drops of rain pocked the wind-ruffled
surface of the canal. The mules hung their heads and tried to
turn their backsides to the storm.

Martha poked her head out of the cabin. "What's wrong,
Tim? Why are we stopping? Don't you want to try to get out of
this storm?"

"It's Adam," the captain shouted over the wind. "And we can't
outrun the storm. We'll stop here 'til the worst is past."

"Will!" Adam panted as he pounded along the towpath. "Give
me . . . a hand up!"

Will leaned over the side of the *Dolley Madison*. "What if I
miss and you fall in?"

"It . . . won't . . . be . . . the   first . . . time!" Adam   puffed,
reaching for Will's outstretched hand.

Thunder crashed while Brennan unhitched the mules, causing the nervous animals to prance around before crossing the
plank walkway between the towpath and the boat. Brennan,
talking softly, calmed them and led them into their stalls. Then
he put Patrick, a bit pink around the eyes and still sniffing now
and then, to work wiping down the wet animals.

Adam and Will followed Luke and Tim into the Callahans' living quarters, where Will slammed the door against the wind and
Adam wiped his face with an equally wet shirttail.

The captain laughed at the boys' streaming faces. "Nice night
for a stroll." He glanced at the women busy putting supper
together and his voice lost its merry tone.

"What made you decide that you wanted to catch up? I
thought you were going to keep an eye out for Hudson's team and

wagon and bring them back in the morning. Here, dry yourself a bit," he said, tossing dry rags at Adam and Will.

"I was going to," Adam said breathlessly. His eyes were round and dark and his face was red from running. Water dripped off the end of his nose and droplets caught in his tight curls and sparkled in the lamplight. "But, I had a feeling that what I heard was more important." Not at all like the "quiet boy-o" that usually worked silently around the *Dolley Madison,* he turned to Luke and said, "Don't worry about your team, Mr. Hudson, I left them in Dr. Ayres' stable. He said that he would bring them out tomorrow when he comes to check on the little girls."

"So, tell me, boy," the captain said to Adam, his voice tight. "Is what I heard true?"

Adam, his chest still heaving from his dash from town, glanced over his shoulder at Will and looked questioningly at the captain.

"You may speak freely."

"I stopped to get a drink at the well the same time they were watering their horses. They're real slave catchers, all right," Adam said. "And by the sound of it, they've had plenty of practice."

"I thought so," Callahan said, handing him a cup of water. "I reckon they've got the town all in an uproar by now."

Adam gulped thirstily, then wiped his upper lip with his forearm. "Well sir, they were at O'Dillon's Saloon this afternoon and talkin' about getting' up a search party, but they musta got some sort of word, because they just up and left. Took off at a mad run. About ran me down, they was in such a hurry."

Suddenly, Will remembered the horses thundering down the street toward Emaline, and Tessa jumping out to pull her to safety. He remembered the animals snorting and grunting as they galloped by, their pounding hooves churning up clouds of dust. He also remembered the thick, black beard and hard, cold eyes of one of the riders.

He jerked.

"What is it, Will?" Brennan asked.

"Uh . . . nothing." Will said.

Callahan nodded thoughtfully. "I've seen some rough characters in my day, but I've heard that this pair has been at it for a long time. They know their business and they aren't going to let anything get in their way, even children, it seems. Have you any other news, boy?"

"Just that no one's seen anyone like the people described on the flyers, either."

"Or, if they have, no one is speakin' of it. Poor souls, I wish 'em speed and a safe harbor," Callahan said, lifting the window curtain and peering out, almost as if he were searching for something, or someone.

After a while, the storm muttered and grumbled off to the east, leaving behind night and the gentle patter of a summer rain. Callahan listened for a moment. "The rain's lessened somewhat. I say we get the *Dolley* back to the lock."

It wasn't long until the *Dolley Madison* reached Lock 32 and the Hudsons' neat, brick house. Adam and Brennan, along with Patrick, who was sound asleep in a pile of fresh straw in a corner of the stable, stayed with the boat while the Callahans and Will helped Eva and Luke settle Emaline and Tessa in the house.

"Will, would you take this candle and go upstairs and bring down the feather bed?" Eva asked. "I think we'll just make a pallet down here for the girls for tonight. They'll be cooler and more comfortable."

Will took the candleholder and headed up the steps.

"Be careful about dripping that beeswax," Eva cautioned. "It is almost impossible to get up once it sticks to something."

Will nodded and straightened the candlestick. He was about halfway up to the loft when a familiar sharp odor met his nose. It grew stronger as he climbed. It was the same sour smell that had surrounded the crowd gathered in Junction that afternoon. The air reeked of sweat and clothing soiled with long wear and badly in need of laundering. His steps slowed, but his heart sped up. Holding the candle high over his head to spread its feeble, dancing light as far as possible, he poked his head into the loft. Nothing looked to be out of place. Will quickly scooped up the bedding Eva had asked for and turned toward the stairs. Then he heard it.

He stopped. He wasn't sure from what direction of the room the sound had come. In one corner sat Mrs. Hudson's fancy hump-backed trunk along with several barrels and some stacked crates—it was a good place for something, or someone, to hide. It was just the tiniest scrape, but even with people talking and moving around downstairs, he'd heard it. The hairs on the back of his neck stiffened and sweat prickled under his arms. Still holding the candle overhead and without taking his eyes from the dark corner, Will squatted and laid the featherbed on the floor. He stood, then carefully, step by step, sliding his feet so as not to cause the floorboards to shift and creak, worked his way toward the other side of the room. As he drew closer the candle gradually brightened the dark corner.

Although he almost hoped he would hear it again, to prove it wasn't his imagination, when the noise did come, Will's stomach clenched and his throat went dry. He stopped short of leaping into the air with a yelp and making a dash for the stairs. The scraping sound was definitely coming from inside the trunk. Because his heart was thumping so hard, he was surprised he could hear anything besides its pounding in his ears.

Mice, he thought. It's probably mice. Some really, really big mice . . . rats, maybe.

Will swallowed hard and reached for the clasp on the trunk. A dark figure suddenly lunged at him from behind the barrels.

Will leaped backward with a sharp intake of air. The candle and holder clattered to the floor and skidded away, plunging the loft into darkness.

A hand came out of the darkness, grabbed his forearm, and held it in a firm grasp.

"Please," a deep voice whispered. "Please, suh."

"Will?" Eva's voice came up the stairs. "Did you drop that candle?"

The hand tightened on Will's arm. "Please, suh, my family," the man whispered. "We heard this here was a safe house."

"Uh, yeah," Will, his voice a thin squeak, called out in answer to Eva. "I . . . I did."

Footsteps sounded on the stairs and a hand holding an oil lamp appeared, followed by Luke's head.

"Will?" He said, looking around. "Need any . . ." Luke halted.

As the weak light of the lamp played over the beams and dark recesses of the attic, it gleamed off the man's black, sweat-beaded face. His thick fingers still held Will's arm in a tight grip.

Will stared at Luke, wide-eyed. "He's . . . lost . . . I think," Will stammered.

"My family, suh. I have to save my family," the man said hoarsely. He turned, and reaching behind a barrel, drew out a small woman. She stood silently in the feeble light. Her eyes were as fearful as her husband's.

Luke slowly approached and held the lamp closer in order to examine the man. Above a black, wiry beard and a wide nose, his dark eyes glistened with fear.

"No, not lost," Luke said. "They're in the right place."

"Eva," Luke called over his shoulder, never taking his eyes from the people standing in his attic. His voice was measured and even. "Get the girls settled and then come up here straight away.

"Well now, I would, if I had that featherbed!" Eva said. "What are you two doing up there? Having a quilting bee?"

"My land," Martha laughed up the stairs. "Do you need any help?"

"Take that bed down to her," Luke directed Will with a jerk of his head.

Will scrambled down the stairs and fell into the kitchen.

"My land!" Martha laughed as Will tumbled down the last few steps.

Luke's voice came down again. "Send up Callahan," he said.

With a puzzled look on his face, the captain climbed into the loft.

"What is it, Mama?" Emaline asked sleepily.

"Oh, you know how sometimes storms cause the roof to leak," Eva said as she spread the mattress out on the floor and helped the girls onto the makeshift bed. "You just close those sleepy eyes and rest."

Eva stood back, watching as Emaline turned on her side with a sigh and closed her eyes. Then briskly gathering her long skirts, Eva started up. "I want to see what is going on up there!" She said.

"My land!" Martha breathed softly when she, following Eva, climbed into the loft. "My land."

When Tom Brown was sure that he and his wife had reached a place of temporary safety, he pulled a tattered rag out of his back pocket, sank weakly to the floor and mopped his face. "I thought we was in the wrong place and caught for sure," he said. "I don't know as we could take it, goin' back, after makin' it this far north. This is my wife, Susan."

"Praise be," Susan said.

A scuffling sound came from the trunk, the same noise Will had first heard when he climbed the stairs. He stepped closer, and flipping the ornate latch on the trunk, lifted the heavy lid. It was too dark to see to the bottom.

"Can I use that lamp for a second?" he asked Luke.

Wordlessly, as everyone looked on, Luke handed the lantern to Will, who held it above the chest. A bundle of rags huddled in the bottom.

"You kin come out now, Ivy," Tom said softly.

Slowly the little pile of clothing came to life. Two small hands clasped the edge of the trunk and a girl about Emaline's size pulled herself upright. She cringed and pulled away as Luke reached to lift her out of the trunk.

"It's alright, Sugar," Tom said, picking the child up and setting her down on the floor where she staggered and plopped onto her bottom.

Eva gasped and leaned over the little girl. "The poor little thing, she's too weak to stand."

To everyone's surprise, Ivy started to giggle and wiggle her feet.

"Pin's n' needles," she said to her mother. "I jest couldn't hold still no longer, 'cuz I gots pins n' needles in my feet!"

Will couldn't help but laugh and like the storm that had blown away the hot, sultry day, it released the fear and tension in the attic of the lockkeeper's house.

Chapter Fifteen

Eva and Martha fixed the Browns something to eat while the men mapped out a plan to help the family on their way. Ivy's spoon clinked steadily against her bowl as she ate fried eggs and cornbread. Martha stood by with a skillet, making sure that no one had to wait for another helping.

"Our son, James, he come this way in the spring," Susan Brown said in her soft Southern accent. "James' goin' to meet us. He s'posed to have a place for us in Ontario. We jest have to get to port in Toledo. There's a ship captain there. He takes people into Canada."

It wasn't long before people talking and moving around wakened Emaline and Tessa in the makeshift bed on the floor. Tessa watched dully through half-open lids. Bursting with curiosity, Emaline sat up immediately despite the bump on her head. She was used to all sorts of people passing the house while traveling on the canal. But the lockkeeper's daughter's interest in the constant parade never dulled. Her eyes widened and her mouth fell open when she spotted the Brown family. With a quick intake of breath, she started to ask her mother a question.

"Mama, who are . . . ?" she asked.

Eva put her finger to her lips, a signal to her daughter to keep questions to herself. Emaline slumped a little, but kept quiet. Sometimes her mother would answer her questions later; sometimes she said "it wasn't something little girls needed to know."

Seeing that Tessa was awake, Will came over and sat beside her. He excitedly began to explain his discovery in the attic, making no mention of his impulse to make a run for it. Emaline scootched closer to hear Will's report.

93

"I bet you about wet your pants," Tess said when Will told of Thomas Brown's hand coming out of the dark. Her words were muffled, but a small spark was returning to her eyes.

"I did not," Will said defensively.

"Well, I would have," Tessa said.

"I jumped about a mile high, though," Will admitted.

"Ooh, I would have just had to scream," Emaline added with a little shiver of excitement. "What about Patrick? Did he miss everything, too?"

"He's asleep on the boat. Captain Tim went out to make sure no other boats were heading toward the lock and he checked on him while he was out there. He says it's lucky we had this storm, because it isn't likely that any boats will be traveling until morning."

Tessa nodded and winced.

"How's your mouth?" Will asked.

"I think the swelling is going down," she said. "I don't know what herb Martha put on it, but it really does seemed to have helped some."

"At least it wasn't goose grease," Will said with a grin.

"For that I am thankful," Tess said, trying to smile, but the pain made her decide against it.

"Will, would you like a piece of this cornbread?" Eva called across the room.

"Yes, please, I would," Will said, getting up. "I guess I'm pretty hungry."

"We've all had quite a day, haven't we?" Eva said. "Tessa? Would you care for some?"

Tessa shook her head carefully and said, "May I have a drink of water?"

"I'll get it for you," Will said.

Emaline squirmed out from under the quilt as her curiosity drew her to the little girl sitting at the table. Having worked her way across the room Emaline squeezed into a chair at the table. Chin in hand, she stared at Ivy, whose spoon was moving rapidly from plate to mouth as bite after bite of food disappeared.

"Mama," Emaline said, "I think this little girl don't get 'nuff to eat."

The murmur of voices stopped and the room fell silent. Ivy slowly laid the spoon beside her bowl and buried her head in her mother's shoulder.

"Why, of course she didn't get enough to eat today, goosey!" Eva said hurriedly. "She's been on a long hike and didn't have time. And you yourself know that nothing tastes better after a long walk than fresh-baked cornbread and a cup of milk!" Eva sent a warm smile in Ivy's direction. "Eat up, child, there's plenty for everyone."

Eva looked sternly at her daughter, pressing her lips tightly together. Emaline's cheeks flushed with a sudden flare of red and she looked down. Ivy stared at her mother, her eyes wide.

"Go on, you eat." Susan urged her daughter. "The Lord doth provide, but we don' always know when it's gonna be. Bes' eat while you can."

Conversation picked up again as the child resumed eating. Tom Brown, talking with Luke and Captain Tim, traced out the route his family had traveled up through Tennessee, Kentucky and across the Ohio River.

"Tess?" Will said quietly, handing her a mug of water.

She gingerly brought the cup to her mouth and sipped. "Yeah?"

"Those men who almost ran you down today, they were slave catchers," he said. "They mean business. They're looking for the Browns."

"Do you think they'll come here and get them?" Tessa said.

"I don't know," he said. "I wonder where they'll go from here. I wonder if the Captain will take them on the boat. That would be cool."

"I don't know," Tessa said. "They can't just stroll down Main Street, that's for sure."

"Tess," Will said, "I'm not so sure this is just a dream anymore. If it's the real thing, those people are in real danger."

"I'm scared," Tessa said. "Sometimes dreams turn into nightmares."

Sometimes it felt as if the days she spent at the Hudson's house were a dream, Tessa thought the next morning. The day before—a dark whirlpool of excitement, fear and pain—seemed like a true nightmare.

It was still early when Dr. Ayres knocked briskly on the Hudson's door. "They are almost as good as new, Mrs. Hudson," he told Eva as he wound strips of clean white rag around Emaline's head, tying it in a firm knot. He was in a hurry to check on the rest of his many patients and was getting ready to leave when Tessa was surprised to hear Aunt Eva telling the doctor about the Browns.

Seeing the girl's eyes grow wide with alarm, Eva turned to her.

"Tessa, don't trouble yourself," she said. "Dr. Ayres is of no danger to the Browns." Turning back to the physician, she said, "They were quite hungry, tired and dirty. They washed up and had a good meal both last night and this morning, but there wasn't time to spare. I had a little dress that Emaline has just outgrown for the child, but not much else. They all seem to be in good health, even though they have no shoes, bless them. However, we thought you might want to check on them."

Emaline motioned Tessa over to a corner, stood on tiptoe and whispered into the taller girl's ear.

"Peas is about delishus," Emaline said.

Tessa stood back and stared at the girl.

"*What?*"

Emaline tried again.

"*Peas abbott pinch nest?*" Tessa repeated what she'd heard, her face wrinkling with confusion.

Emaline stamped her foot on the floor in frustration, grabbed Tessa's sleeve and yanked her closer.

"He's an *abolitionist!*" Emaline hissed loudly.

Dr. Ayres laughed. "Emaline is trying to tell you, with a great deal of tact, I must say, that I am an abolitionist."

"Emaline!" Eva spat out sternly. "Haven't I told you over and over that whispering *and* interrupting are rude!"

Emaline's face, already pink, deepened to rose.

"Oh, say now," Dr. Ayres said, smiling down at the girl, "the child's just excited. After all, things have been rather up in the air around here the past few days."

Turning to Tessa he said, "Surely you've heard of abolition, young lady?"

"Abolition. Oh, yeah, sure I have," Tessa said. "I just couldn't understand what Emaline was saying."

"I believe that slavery should be abolished—made illegal— everywhere, in every state," Dr. Ayres explained to Tessa, "not only in the North." He shook his head sadly. "It was a tragic day when that new fugitive law was enacted. Set us back decades. I predict it will end in not just one tragedy, but many. Even people who have lived their entire lives in freedom here in the North have been snatched off the streets and taken south against their will." He shook his head sadly. "This could be the beginning of the end of the United States. Imagine America split asunder."

Tessa rapidly subtracted in her head. It's only 1850. The Civil War started in 1861 and ended in 1865. But it won't happen for 11 years, she thought. And what he's predicting almost came true because the United States was "split asunder" for four years.

"Eva," Dr. Ayres said as he opened the door, "I must be on my way." He sighed as he closed up his bag. "There's an outbreak of fever among some of the canalers rooming in Junction. I heard there were a couple of cases of typhoid along the canal in Defiance last week. In fact, one family lost two children to it. I pray that whatever it is sickening those men in Junction is just a summer complaint and not typhoid or cholera. We do not need an epidemic." He stepped onto the wide stone step outside the door and tapped his tall, black hat onto his head. "I don't know what people expect when they dump their chamber pots into one side of the canal and dip drinking water from the other. I'm cautioning people not to drink from the town well, either. I'll step aboard the *Dolley* and check on the family before I go. As for the fever, I suggest you and your family restrict your visits to Junction for now."

Emaline and Tessa crowded together at the window and watched the tall, thin doctor walk briskly toward the lock and board the boat, then follow Captain Tim into the cargo hold.

Brennan appeared, leading two of the mules. Patrick trotted behind. Tessa hadn't had the heart to admit to her little cousin that she couldn't tell one mule from the other. When Emaline saw Patrick, she rapped on the window and waved wildly when he looked up. Patrick turned away from the girls as two riders on horseback arrived. They dismounted and one handed Brennan a flyer while the other pointed with his shotgun, first toward the *Dolley*, then toward the house. Tessa's mouth went dry as she recognized the men who had almost trampled Emaline. Tessa hadn't gotten a good look at either one of the riders in the confusion of the day before. Today she saw that one was tall and slender and younger than the other, but they looked as if they could be brothers, or maybe father and son.

Tessa eased the girl away from the window and when Emaline protested, shushed her. Emaline's lower lip went out and her face darkened. Tessa had never spoken sharply to her before.

"Aunt Eva!" Tessa whispered loudly. "It's them! Those guys! The . . . the slave catchers!"

"Ivy!" Emaline wailed.

"Hush now! She's fine," Eva said. "Come away from there!" She quickly looked around the room, making sure no sign of the Browns had been left behind. Their few ragged belongings had been rolled into a small pack, tied with a frayed rope and slung over Thomas' shoulder.

Tessa couldn't stand it another minute and slid over to the window and peeked through the curtains. Soon Eva and Emaline joined her. The older of the two riders was talking angrily to Brennan while Patrick, wide-eyed, petted one of the mules, who nervously tossed her head. Adam and Will stood on the deck blocking the entrance to the boat. The younger slave catcher put one booted foot on the gangplank just as Dr. Ayres climbed up out of the hold and stepped on deck, tapping his tall hat into place. He was smiling, but as soon as he saw the strangers, his face dropped and his shoulders sagged. Pulling a white kerchief from his waistcoat, he made a big show of mopping his forehead and the back of his neck. Then the doctor passed slowly by the men, then stopped at the door of the cabin and set his bag down. Opening it, he took out a poster and a small hammer, dug in his pocket, brought out some nails and proceeded to tack the sign to the door. By this time the older slave catcher had pushed his way through Adam and Will. Tessa could see the man's lips moving as he, squinting, read the large black print.

DIPTHERIA QUARANTINE!
These Premises Are Under Quarantine
No Person shall be permitted to enter, leave, or take any article, nor remove this placard from this house without written legal consent under full penalty of the law.
Animals must not be permitted to leave these premises.
Penalty is a fine of not less than $10 or more than $100 or to be imprisoned for a period of not less than 10 days or more than 30 days or both at the discretion of the Court.

Luke, Tim, Adam and Brennan had spent most of the night arranging crates, boxes and barrels to create a small, hidden cave for the Browns. Patrick slept peacefully through the night, unaware of the activity below decks. As soon as the Browns had a quick breakfast, Captain Tim had hurried them into the tiny hiding place. They would stay there, tucked away in the hold of the *Dolley Madison,* all the way to Toledo, only coming out on deck late at night for fresh air. If the man who piloted a ship between the United States and Canada could be found, the Browns would travel to safety on a swift sailing clipper ship.

"Are those men still there?" Aunt Eva whispered to Tessa.

Tessa peered through the thin cloth and whispered back, "Yes. The one with the beard is talking to the doctor."

The three of them peeked through the curtains again. Doctor Ayres was looking sadly toward the house and shaking his head. He removed his hat and held it over his heart.

A look of alarm washed over the younger man's face and he hurried to his horse and mounted. Angrily kicking the horse's sides, he wheeled around and headed south. The older man stepped up to Dr. Ayres' and stared into his face. Dr. Ayres shrugged helplessly and looked up to the heavens. Then he made a little waving motion with his hands, as if the man was a chicken being shooed out of a garden. Tessa and Emaline giggled. The man stomped off the boat, shoving Will out of his way as he left.

After the older slave catcher followed his partner and had ridden out of sight, Dr. Ayres popped his hat back on his head, took the sign down and put it back in his bag. Whistling, he climbed into his carriage, tipped his hat to the crew of the Dolley Madison, and left.

Soon after, pulled by Polly and Pearl, the boat slid slowly away, headed for Defiance. From there the *Dolley* would continue north to Toledo. Brennan and Patrick guided the mules, while Adam and Will busily swept and scrubbed the narrow decks. Martha sat in a shady spot and snapped off the stem ends of green beans that had come from Eva Hudson's garden. Captain Tim was at the tiller. It was just like any other morning on the canal. This time though, the boat carried a secret. If the wrong people discovered it, it would mean the end of freedom, and possibly worse, for the Browns and jail and large fines for the Callahans, their crew and anyone else who had come to the Browns' aid.

Slowly, as the day warmed and brightened, the gloomy feelings left over from the night before disappeared. Tessa's near collision with the slave catchers had left her bruised and aching, but the warmth of the sun as it fell across the Hudson's table and onto her shoulders felt good on her sore muscles. She carefully guided a spoonful of oatmeal past her puffy lip. Although Tessa's lip felt as fat and round as a balloon, Emaline promised her that it didn't look at all that bad.

"Hurry, Tessa!" Emaline hung over the back of a chair, impatiently urging Tessa to finish eating. The little girl was bouncing with energy, not at all bothered by the fact that she had nearly been trampled to death the day before. The thin band of white cloth the doctor wrapped around her head had already slipped sideways over one eye, making her look more like a pirate than a patient.

"I wish Ivy could have stayed and played some more, don't you, Tessa?" Emaline said, holding her skirt out and swaying back and forth as she watched her shadow dance on the floor.

Before Tessa had a chance to answer, Eva whirled around.

"Emaline!" She said. "You cannot mention Ivy. We explained that to you. I thought you were old enough to understand how important it is that you make no mention of the Browns."

Emaline's face crumpled and tears pooled in her large eyes. "I'm sorry, Mama. I'm sorry. It's just that . . ."

"I know, I know," Eva said softly. She wiped her hands on her apron and walked over to her daughter and put her hands on Emaline's small shoulders. "We *were* just talking about them with Dr. Ayres. That was different. He can help them. But, if you really care about Ivy and her mother and father, then you must not breathe another word about them. Their lives depend upon it."

Tears slipped one after another down Emaline's face. "I didn't mean no harm, Mama. Honest I didn't."

Her mother took a small handkerchief from the pocket of her apron and dabbed at the tears on Emaline's face. "*Any* harm, dear. Not '*no harm*.' Of course you didn't. You must understand that living here on the lock as we do, many, many people pass through on the canal. Not all of them feel the same way as we do about helping runaways. Some people wouldn't hesitate to turn in a little child and her parents for that reward money. We don't know who we can trust."

"Now!" Eva said briskly, giving Emaline a hug, "That storm really cooled things off last night, so you may go outside and play quietly this morning. You must rest this afternoon, though."

As they closed the door, Eva called, "You girls stay away from the canal! The good Lord only knows what will happen next!"

Chapter Sixteen

Will took a deep breath and let it out shakily as the older of the slave hunters rode off. Although the morning was cool, sweat filmed his forehead and dampened the back of his neck. Everyone else on board looked and acted as if it were any other morning on the canal and the only cargo in the hold was a load of cordwood. Will had always hungered for excitement and adventure, but now that he was in the middle of it, his insides jumped at every crackle in the underbrush. What if they came back? At any moment, he expected the slave catchers to return and charge the *Dolley Madison,* waving guns and demanding to search the boat in spite of the doctor's quarantine sign. What would he do if something happened to Patrick? Or Tessa?

Cupping his hands around his eyes to block out the morning sun, he strained to see a far as he could down the towpath. It was empty. He wasn't sure how much power the Fugitive Slave Act gave the bounty hunters. He had a feeling that it didn't matter to Captain Tim and that he wouldn't allow a search of the *Dolley Madison* without a struggle. Will had seen the captain's shotgun hanging on the wall in the cabin. He also knew that Brennan carried a small flintlock pistol tucked into the wide leather sash tied around his waist. Will didn't think Brennan would be slow to use it, either.

What was going to happen when they got to port on Lake Erie? Will wondered. Would those men have turned around and taken another route to Toledo, knowing that the fugitives were fleeing northward? Maybe there was another, safer way for the Browns to make their escape into Canada?

Brennan clicked his tongue against his teeth and Pearl, the lead mule, then Polly, hitched directly behind her, leaned into the harness. The towrope slowly reeled out, and pulled taut, sending a spray of water into air that caught the early sun in a shower of rainbow drops. The *Dolley Madison* slipped away from Lock 32, headed for Toledo.

Under his wide-brimmed straw hat, Patrick's face was solemn as he trailed behind the gruff driver. Will could tell by the dreamy look on his brother's face that the boy believed he was really guiding the animals along the towpath. Will had seen plenty of children—their bare feet caked in the dust of the towpath—driving mule teams. Boys and girls alike served as crewmembers of family owned boats and many were younger than Patrick. The difference, Will thought, was those kids had grown up on the water, their first steps taken on the deck of a canal boat. The tiniest ones spent their days tethered to boats with a rope tied around their middles to prevent them from falling overboard and drowning. The older kids fished and swam in the water every chance they got. The canal was truly the only life many of them had ever known.

When Brennan saw Will watching Patrick, he cast a quick look over his shoulder at the child padding along behind, then back at Will. The gruff man's few teeth gleamed out of his wild, dark beard as he grinned and winked at Will.

"We'll make a right canawler out of 'im yet, we will," Brennan said. "That boy's got a way with the hinnies, he does. It's natural born, I reckon."

"Hinnies?" Will asked.

"My girls," Brennan said. "Pearl and Polly, Prudence and Mae. They're the envy of many on the Big Ditch, ya know."

Down in the hold, Ivy Brown settled onto her mother's lap and sighed.

"I wish I could look out the window. I wish I could walk the mules, Ma, like that other boy. It's hot in here an' I got pins and needles in my feet agin."

"Now it seems to me that just yesterday somebody I know was complainin' about how tired she was, doin' all that walkin' and how she never, ever wanted to walk a towpath again," her mother said. "Day or night."

"Someday soon, you gonna run and play and look out all you want," Tom said. "Just got to be patient, girl."

As Susan set to work combing out the child's hair with her fingers, the girl relaxed, laid her head against her mother's shoulder and closed her eyes.

"Ma?" she asked sleepily.

"Yes, baby," Susan said.

"Do you ever git afraid?"

"No, baby, I don't get afraid," Susan answered. Her hands, caught in the tangle of black curls, stopped. She looked over her daughter's head and her eyes locked with her husband's.

"I'm glad of that, 'cuz if you and Pa was to be scared, then maybe I might be, too."

"Once we get to Canady, we ain't gonna have nothing to be afraid of 'cept gitting the bellyache from eating too much apple pie," Tom said.

Susan resumed combing through Ivy's hair. "Oh my," she said, "too much apple pie."

"I don't believe I could ever, ever eat too much apple pie," Ivy said.

Up on the house, Tim Callahan leaned on the tiller and scanned the sky. It was cloudless except for a few wispy mares' tails high overhead. He figured the clear weather would last at least another day or two. When the sun settled in the west that night, a full moon would rise. The countryside would be almost bright as day when its silver light poured down. Boating on moonlit nights was not uncommon, but was usually undertaken by boats with at least three mule teams. Traveling around the clock would be tiring for both his mules and his crew, but this cargo was not only in danger, they were dangerous to have on board. He had no way of knowing the slave catchers' whereabouts, so it was best to just keep moving, which left him little choice but to take the *Dolley* northward through the night. This wasn't the first time runaway slaves had used the towpaths to travel to safety. Callahan also knew that with the help of his Martha and their trusted crew, he would risk everything again to help someone to freedom.

Once the Dolley was well away from Lock 32, Will relaxed a little and his stomach began to feel less like it was home to a family of lively squirrels. He knew Martha and Tim had explained to Patrick how important it was not to tell anyone about the family hidden in the cargo hold. But Will wanted to make sure his brother really understood that this secret meant the difference between a life of freedom or slavery for the Browns. Will grabbed Patrick as he rounded the corner of the mules' stall.

"You know how many times I've told you not to talk about where we come from and how we got here?" Will said.

Patrick nodded. His thin arms and square hands were brown, the once soft palms hardened by working with the mules. His feet were equally brown and it was hard to tell where the dirt started and stopped. He looked suspiciously out from under the wide brim of his hat.

"Yeah, I remember. I ain't said nothin'. I'm not a baby. You don't have to keep tellin' me over and over."

"I know. I know you're not a baby. That's not what I meant," Will said. "But this is even bigger than that. It's not just the Browns. Captain Tim and Luke, Adam, even that doctor and the Hudsons could go to jail if anyone finds out about this."

Patrick's voice was low and firm when he answered.

"Will, I know that. You don't have to explain every little thing to me, you know. I tol' ya, I'm not a baby. In fact, Brennan's going to let me handle the mules all by myself this afternoon. He needs to get some rest since we're gonna to be traveling through the night."

Will was shocked into silence and stopped walking for a second. Brennan was going to trust one of his prized mule teams to Patrick. Suddenly his little brother seemed much older than his eight short years. He took a couple of long strides and caught up with Patrick, who had not missed a step.

"So, which one is Polly and which one's Pearl?" Will asked, patting a mule's nose.

Bullfrogs thrummed their rubber band song in the dark, plopping into the canal with loud splashes as the plodding hooves of the lead mule drew near. The air was warm and damp and ghostly tendrils of fog coiled upward from the water. From over-head the full moon was a small silver coin in the sky. The insect chorus was deafening and mosquitoes buzzed in a cloud around Will's head, but he still jumped at every rustle in the underbrush.

The *Dolley Madison* was steadily making her way northward through the darkness of night. He had no idea of the time, but Will figured it had to be well past midnight. His shoulder ached, so he switched the heavy lantern to the other hand. Although he fought it, his eyes watered, and a yawn so big it hurt escaped.

Patrick was fast asleep, sprawled on Mae's back, his head resting on her neck, his arms and legs swaying gently. At night-fall, when Martha had suggested that Patrick come into the cabin and go to bed, he'd politely refused, pointing out that Brennan needed his help. The captain had laughed and told Martha to "quit mollycoddling the boy-o."

As the hours drew on and Patrick could no longer keep his eyes open and he finally stumbled, Brennan scooped the boy up and gently placed him on Mae's back. Patrick's feet stuck out from under the blanket Brennan had tossed over the sleeping boy. Will wrinkled his nose. Patrick carried the smell of mules with him all the time now. Sleeping on one under a blanket reek-ing of the animals' sweat would only intensify the odor. If his lit-tle brother began munching hay, it wouldn't surprise him a bit.

All the same, Will thought about his slumbering brother with envy. He was so tired, even a bed on a mule's back would have felt like heaven. Jumpy and tense all day, his muscles were tight and sore. It felt like a week had passed since morning. He was couldn't believe how calm the rest of the crew was. Other than the unusual quiet that hung over the *Dolley,* there was no clue that the very people for whom the slave catchers, with big guns and the law on their side, were scouring the countryside, were stowed away in the hold. Will hopped on his right foot for a moment, and dug at a mosquito bite near his left ankle.

Captain Tim's voice came out of the darkness. "Hey, William! Are ye havin' difficulties? What are ye doin' up there? Tryin' to teach that lantern a reel? It's bobbin' about like it like ye'd asked it to dance."

"No, sir," Will answered, putting both feet back on the tow-path. "Just scratching."

Will stood up and continued walking along the towpath, swat-ting at the pesky insects as they whined in his ears. He wished a good stiff breeze would spring up and keep the bugs away. It probably doesn't matter if those guys catch up to us or not, he thought, we'll all have malaria before the night is over. That's probably what's wrong with Adam now, he thought.

Late in the afternoon, Martha had noticed Adam slumped on the deck, resting his head on his knees. He held a rag to his nose.

"I don't know, ma'am," he replied when she asked if he was feeling poorly. "I got this nosebleed that just don't seem to want to stop. And," he shivered, "I just can't seem to get warm."

"Can't get warm?" Martha squinted up at the blazing sun. It was a typical July day—hot and humid, with very little air to stir the limply hanging leaves.

Martha stepped closer to Adam and peered into his face. She reached out and placed the back of her hand on his forehead. His face, usually brown as an acorn in autumn, was pale and waxy. He shivered. She sent him to his bunk below deck. At supper he'd refused the food she took him, even though it was his favorite, beans and cornbread with molasses. Will noticed the worried looks that passed between Martha and the captain.

Since Adam had not been well enough, Will was leading the *Dolley* through the longest night of his life. After several hours of straining to see into the darkness, his eyes burned and his neck and shoulders ached. The candle in the heavy lantern he carried cast a feeble glow. It was almost useless against the trailing mists and swarms of mosquitoes that rose up from the canal. He forgot about slave catchers as weariness finally forced him to give up trying to see more than a foot or two ahead at a time. He plodded along like the mules, half asleep, thinking only of how good it would feel to lay his head on a pillow. Life on the canal was no longer fun. It was a punishment.

A crackling sound in the underbrush brought him instantly awake. He listened intently, but didn't hear it again. I must have dreamed it, he thought. I think I'm actually walking in my sleep. He shook himself and rubbed his eyes. Behind him Brennan was talking softly to the mules. A steady chorus of night creatures— crickets, katydids, and tree frogs throbbed from the trees and grasses, but Will didn't hear the noise again.

He didn't know how long he had been trudging along, just managing to put one foot in front of the other. As the night dragged on, the muggy air cooled and his shirt began to cling damply to his thin shoulders. He shivered. When Will heard quick footsteps from behind, he stopped, and holding the lantern high, turned around.

Martha, a knitted shawl thrown over her head, was hurrying toward him. Tiny droplets of mist clung to the curls that framed her kind face.

"I thought you might be getting a mite weary and a little cold. Here," she said, wrapping a small quilt around Will.

"Give me the lantern for a while," she said.

Will tried to uncurl his stiff fingers from around the iron ring of the lantern. For a moment his hand wouldn't obey.

"Poor thing," Martha said. "You ought to go back and get some rest."

"I'm okay," Will lied as he painfully opened and closed his stiff hands. He changed the subject. "How did you get off the boat? We haven't stopped."

Martha laughed lightly. "I didn't grow up on the canal without learning a trick or two. My pa had a boat down by Cincinnati. My ma was a cook and that's how they met. From the time I was a little girl, there hasn't yet been a boat that would go so fast I couldn't jump off when I wanted to."

"Well, I should hold that lantern," Will said. "The captain's depending on me since Adam is sick."

"I've walked many a mile on a dark towpath, too," Martha said. "Here's a piece of leftover cornbread. I figgered you must be pretty hungry by now."

As they walked along, Will took a bite of bread. He *was* hungry.

"It's almost dawn," Martha said, motioning toward the east with the lantern. "It's always coldest this time of day."

Will was amazed to see that the sky had lightened from black to slate blue. The moon was gone and only a few stars shone above the fog that had thickened into a ghostly blanket that hovered over the canal. The night chorus of insects had quieted, and birds chirped a few sleepy notes.

"We'll take time when it's full light to have a right proper breakfast." Martha's voice grew serious. "And perhaps try to find a doctor for Adam."

Will turned back from the dawn sky and said, "He's not any better?"

"I've just come from Adam. He's asleep now, but he's burning up with fever and hasn't been able to keep anything down," Martha said. "Susan said she would sit with him while I came out to check on you."

Just then the crackle that had jarred Will awake in the night came again. It sounded like something . . . or someone . . .

creeping through the tall weeds growing by the canal embankment. This time there was a long, thin, drawn out cry with it—a cross between a whine and a growl.

"Did you hear that?" Martha whispered to Will.

Will shivered again, only partly from the early morning chill. At his feet lay the half-eaten piece of bread he had dropped when startled by the eerie cry.

Chapter Seventeen

A few days after their close call with the slave catchers, Tessa and Emaline, as Dr. Ayres had predicted, were as "right as rain." Other than a faint green shadow under her left eye and a small scab on her lower lip, Tessa felt fine. The cut on Emaline's head was only a thin, pink line that traced across her forehead. She bounced around waiting for Tessa to finish eating breakfast.

"I'm ready, Aunt Eva," Tessa said, carrying her dishes over to the tub of dishwater in the dry sink. She hesitated, her manners struggling with her desire to be free. "Would you like me to wash these up for you?"

"No, not today," Eva replied. "Go out and get some sunshine."

"Emaline, do stop leaping about like a spring lamb," her mother said.

"I want to wait for Tessa, Mama," Emaline said, spinning in a circle.

"Did you shake out your feather tick properly?" Her mother asked.

"Well . . ." Emaline said.

"You must fluff up your feather bed or you'll get feather crowns," Eva warned.

"What's a feather crown?" Tessa asked.

"When the feathers in a tick aren't shaken apart, they begin to stick to each other and soon they form hard circles . . . little crowns," Eva replied. "Not all children are fortunate enough to have soft feather ticks on their beds," she said in Emaline's direction. "Many must be content to sleep on either straw or corn husks."

"I'll go do it right away, Mama," Emaline said, starting up the steps.

"I'll help," Tessa said.

"Mama's goose feather ticks are her pride and joy," Emaline explained as she picked up the edge of her comforter and gave it a hard shake. "They were a wedding gift from my grandmother. She raised the geese herself."

"I guess I never really thought about where they came from," Tessa said, patting and smoothing the fat bed cover.

Emaline was already half way down the stairs. "C'mon, Tessa," she called.

As the girls hurried out the door, Eva called. "Don't forget to let the chickens out. And put fresh straw in the nest boxes!"

A lock horn sounded from a distance and Emaline and Tessa started for the door.

"Unless you'd like to help me with your new quilt," Eva added. "I'd really like to get some piecing done on it today, Emaline, and it is high time you learned how to ply a needle."

"I can sew, Mama. I've worked ever so many cross stitch samplers," Emaline said, hopping impatiently from one foot to the other. "Didn't I piece a nine-patch for my doll? I promise I'll help with my quilt, but mightn't we please go out today?"

Eva smiled at the two girls poised for flight. "Yes, go! But don't forget the chickens."

As Emaline and Tessa stepped into the soft morning air, Eva called her usual warning, "Stay out from underfoot at the lock. Stay away from strangers. And keep those chickens out of my garden!"

The day was too clear and fine to spend inside with a needle and thread. The two girls hurried out the door and headed for the chicken coop. When Tessa opened the wooden latch on the door, chickens fluttered out in a flurry of black and white feathers. Squawking, the hens that Eva called her "dominikers," scattered around the yard. Tessa watched as they busily plucked tender green blades of grass and scratched for bugs and tiny snails. She recognized their breed as the Dominique—an old fashioned pioneer chicken according to her 4-H fancy poultry book.

Keeping watch for the big mean rooster Tessa had nicknamed El Diablo, the girls climbed on the swing to see how high they could make it go. From their seats on the swing, they watched and listened to the sights and sounds of a busy day at Lock 32. Some of the boats traveling the canal were empty freighters that

Emaline called "light boats." Often two and three at a time waited for the next turn to go through the lock.

"I'm tired of swinging," Emaline said after a while. "It's making me dizzy. I'm going to go get my tea party things."

"Okay," Tessa said. "I'll go brush off your table."

"Hey-ey! Lo-ock!" A crewman sang out as a boat drew close to the canal.

"That's a freighter and I can tell from here she's fully loaded—maybe with coal or barrels of flour or even dry goods," Emaline said as she set out a saucer with a large triangle broken out of it. "I wish we could go closer, but Papa would just chase us away. He doesn't like to be bothered while he's fittin' the lock and Mama doesn't like for me to be around the canalers."

"Why not?" Tessa said.

"She says that some of them aren't proper folk and that they're too rough for children and ladies to be around. And sometimes they fight," Emaline said as she plucked a long blade of grass from the clump at her feet. She held it between her thumbs, brought it up to her mouth and blew, creating a thin squeak.

"Who fights?" Tessa asked, picking a blade of grass for herself.

"The boatmen. Sometimes if more than one boat gets to the lock at the exact same time, there's a fight to see who gets to go first." Emaline blew on her grass whistle again and smiled with satisfaction at the loud squawk.

"Your mother lets you watch that?" Tessa asked. She picked three more blades of grass and began to braid them together.

"She don't let me watch 'em if she knows," Emaline said, grinning. "But if I stand up on her trunk up in the loft, I can see out the window. And I can hear the ruckus, even through the window glass. And . . ." The girl shivered with delight. "Sometimes there's lots of *blood*. Then they haul the loser off to the side and Mama goes out to tend to 'im as best she can, but sometimes they have to call for the doctor to come out anyway. That doesn't happen very often, though." Emaline sounded disappointed. "Papa don't 'low 'em to get into it much. Says it ain't a respectable way to run a lock." She stood on tiptoe and looked up the canal. "I hope a passenger packet locks through. Lots of times there's ladies dressed up fancy, and Mama usually lets me go out to the lock then. And she comes out, too."

Emaline cupped her hands around her eyes to block the water's glittering glare. "Looks like Pa is keeping things moving this morning. When I grow up I don't want to be a lock tender. I want to be a captain. I want to have my own canal boat, just like Captain Callahan. I'll have a dozen mules and go from Cincinnati to Toledo, faster n' anybody. I'll live on my boat and when the water freezes, I'll put on runners and make her into a sled so I never have to stop, even in the winter."

"That'd be fun," Tessa said. "What would your boat look like?"

"Blue with white shutters. I'll paint her blue top to keel and from deadeye to port. And that's what I'll name her, too." The girl replied, still watching the canal. "I'll call her *Bluebird*. Or maybe *Bluebell*."

"Well, those are pretty names," Tessa said. "What would you carry on your boat? Coal, oats and corn?

"No."

"Cord wood? Chickens?" Tessa plugged her nose and said, "Hogs?"

"No and no, and especially no to pigs!" Emaline said. "I'd let the other captains haul those things. When I boat the canal, I'll carry cakes and candy and toys. An' the mules will wear shiny gold shoes and lots of silver bells, too, so ever'one can hear us coming."

"That sounds like a wonderful boat," Tessa said, smiling.

"And Tess?" Emaline said.

"Yes?"

Emaline looked around then lowered her voice. "Do you s'pose I could carry little children to where it's safe to live like Captain Callahan does?"

"Yes, I think you could do that," Tessa said. "But, who knows. Things have a way of changing for the better sometimes."

"Really?"

"Yeah." Tessa said. "They do. Maybe not as quick as we think they ought to. Most people take a long time to change. But, remember what your mom said about not talking about the Browns?"

"Oh, I know. I won't say things when there's people around," Emaline said. "I just wonder what Ivy's doing now. I wish I was going along. I wish I could of give her something to take along to remember me by."

"They were in a hurry and couldn't take much to carry. It would have slowed them down too much," Tessa said.

"I s'pose so," Emaline said. "Oh and I want to ship books on my boat, too. 'Specially the ones with pictures. I have a storybook. Mama might have let me give Ivy that, but I didn't think of it in time."

"Will likes to draw pictures," Tessa said. "You should have him draw some for you."

"My birthday is next week, maybe he could draw me a picture of my *Bluebird* for my birthday," Emaline said, her eyes shining.

"I tell you what," Tessa said. "If we see him, I'll just happen to mention it. How's that?"

In answer, Emaline grinned widely, blew a long, loud squawk on the blade of grass, then threw her head back and sang out, "He-ey-ey, Lo-ock!"

Tessa laughed at the little girl's perfect imitation of a boatman. Suddenly, gruff, angry voices came from the direction of the lock. Tessa shaded her eyes with her hand and squinted against the sun. Two boats were waiting, one upstream of the lock, headed north, while the other sat with its bow pointed at the angled downstream gates. Two men were in a similar position, nose to nose, with clenched fists at their sides.

"A fight!" Emaline said, throwing down her grass whistle and scrambling to her feet.

The shouts grew louder. "I'll lick ye, I will, ye yaller dog! Ever' body here kin swear to it that we wuz here first." The threat came from a big red-haired man who was leaning over a shorter man.

"It's Rusty Red and Cincy Bill!" Emaline called over shoulder as she hurried toward the canal. "They just *hate* each other!"

The shorter man lacked inches in height, but was wide through the shoulders. He snatched his hat off and threw it to the ground. "I'd like ta see ya try, ya big red ox!" He shoved his sleeves up revealing thick, hairy forearms. Spitting into both palms, he held his fists up in a boxing stance. "Ever'body here knows the *Andrew Jackson* has the right-o-way and I aim ta see to it the *Andrew Jackson* gets through first!"

With Tessa close behind, Emaline skirted around the small yard, keeping well away from the house, and crept through the trees in order to get closer to the action.

"What're they arguing about?" Tessa whispered. She slapped at a mosquito on her cheek, leaving a smear of blood. It was one of many insects that rose in a cloud with each step through the undergrowth.

"The upstream boat's s'posed to have the right of way over a downstream," Emaline whispered over her shoulder. "And a passenger packet's s'posed to have it over a freighter—'cause they're faster. But, it doesn't always work out that way, 'cause some of the captains hire their crew for how big they are and how hard they can hit."

It wasn't long before Luke Hudson broke up the impending fight. He walked quickly into the gathering crowd, a large pole in one hand and a watch in the other.

"All right, fellers, we none of us have any time to waste on this fine day," he said in a friendly voice, yet underneath was a tone that meant he wasn't going to put up with much nonsense. "You all know I don't allow fightin' under my watch. Besides, Rusty, you know Bill has the right o'way, being the upstream boat."

The big red-haired man, shot Luke a look blacker than a thunderstorm, but moved slowly off to wait his proper turn.

Not long after first Cincy Bill's boat, then Rusty Red's passed out of sight, the girls watched as another boat entered the lock from the south. Tessa heard singing and at first thought it was coming from the boat, but as it floated off, the singing got louder instead of softer and she began to make out the words. The music was coming from a southward direction.

"Little Sally Waters, sittin' in the sun . . . weepin', cryin' fer her skipper to come . . . ."

Emaline leaped to her feet, straining to look down the towpath.

"Rise, Sally, rise, wipe yer eyes on yer frock . . . yer little capn's billed fer here . . . ."

There was a dramatic pause, then the voice ended the song with: " . . . an-n-nd . . . at this port will dock!"

Just as the last note faded away, a man came into sight on the towpath. Stepping happily, he turned toward the house. The man was small, almost elf-like, with a wrinkled face. But Tessa couldn't tell if he was old or just weathered, because his lively step made it look as if springs were hidden in his worn boots. He was dressed in leather knee pants and a dark green coat with long tails that fluttered behind him as he walked. A battered blue cap perched on his head and a small white pipe jutted from his mouth. He carried a small but bulging cloth sack.

"Look!" Emaline gasped. She scrambled to her feet. "Look! It's a real live leprechaun! C'mon," she said, grabbing Tessa's hand and pulling her toward the house.

Chapter Eighteen

One moment the cornbread that Martha had given Will lay in the dust at his feet, barely visible in the gray dawn, and the next it was gone. A yellow blur burst from the weeds, dashed under Martha's long skirts, snatched up the bread and ran off. Martha, snatching her skirts up, shrieked and danced a little jig as the creature ran between her feet.

"What was that?" Will shouted.

Captain Tim heard Martha scream. "Hey there!" he called out. "Are ye hurt, Martha?"

"We're fine, Tim," Martha answered. "Hold up for a spell!"

Brennan slowed the mules and Patrick opened his eyes and sat up, instantly awake.

Will skidded down the embankment in the same direction the blur had disappeared.

Martha hurried over to the edge as Will slid down the embankment and headed into the thick woods that edged the canal. "Use care, Will!" she called through the mist.

The fog had settled at the bottom of the berm, making it hard to see. Will listened intently, and thought he heard a twig snap. He followed the sound and came upon a small dog. Having already wolfed the bread down, it was busy licking the crumbs from its paws. Expecting the creature to dash off at any moment, or leap forward and attack, Will spoke softly.

"Hey, fella," he said.

The dog, a half-grown puppy, yelped, jumped backward and cowered. Will slowly offered his hand and the dog didn't run. It crept through the grass on its belly, sniffed at the cornbread crumbs left on Will's fingers and licked them off with a quick, pink tongue.

115

"Why, you're just hungry," Will said.

The puppy whined, rolled on its back, tail waving. His long silky ears, matted with burrs, flopped back.

"Will!" Martha called. "What is it? Be careful it doesn't bite you!"

"It's just a puppy!" He called over his shoulder.

He leaned down and picked up the dog, feeling loose skin slip over the animal's ribs and backbone. The little dog was starving. Its yellow coat was rough and dirty and he smelled. By the time Will climbed back up to the towpath, Patrick was fully awake and jigging around with excitement. He reached out for the pup.

"Can we keep it? Can we? Please?" Patrick said, turning to Martha. "I've always wanted my own dog!"

"We've got Barley," Will blurted without thinking.

"Barley's your dog," Patrick said, as the puppy slathered the boy's face with its tongue.

"You never told us you had a dog," Martha said. "Did you have to leave him behind?" she asked sadly.

"Oh . . . uh . . . we *had* a dog a long time ago . . ." Will said, hurriedly.

"Yeah," Patrick chimed in. "Before we were orphans. Can we please keep this one? Look how skinny he is. He's hungry. He *needs* us."

"Well," she looked helplessly back at her husband. "We'll see."

A grin lit up Brennan's bearded face and he chuckled softly.

"Let's get goin', Martha," Tim called out. "We need to make Providence today. Will, ye can douse that lantern now."

Patrick was face to face with the pup and the little dog's tail lashed happily back and forth as he washed the tip of Patrick's freckled nose.

"Boys, let's get back aboard and see about fixing some breakfast for everyone," Martha said.

"My puppy, too?" Patrick asked.

"Puppy, too," Martha said. "I tell you what, Mr. Patrick, before that animal sets foot in my house, he's going to have a bath!"

Martha, Will and Patrick, holding tight to the pup, walked back to the boat. Brennan, making use of the time, went about switching the mules with the rested team.

"Hey, Will," Brennan called, "since my partner is busy, help the girls aboard, will ye?"

Patrick shoved the puppy into Will's arms and leaped for the bridle. "That's my job," he said. "I'll do it, Brennan."

The pup snuggled in Will's arms and gave a contented sigh. Will watched while Patrick, talking gently to the mules, soberly unhitched the team. Will couldn't believe the change in his brother. Patrick, the same little kid who used any excuse at home to get out of cleaning his hamster cage, willingly spent hours currying, feeding and shoveling up after the mules.

Brennan laughed as he watched Patrick calmly lead the mules over the wooden gangplank and onto the *Dolley Madison*. "What ya gonna name that new hound o' yours?"

"I haven't thought about it," Patrick said, slowing his step. The mule, sensing food and rest just a few steps away, fidgeted.

"What's *your* name?" the boy called out to the mule driver.

"Why, ye know it's Brennan, ye daft boy." the man said, laughing.

"No, no, your *real* name," Patrick said.

"'Tis me real name," Brennan said.

"I think he means your first name," Will said.

At this, the smile left Brennan's face and he shifted uncomfortably. "Er . . . Ever'body knows I go by the name o' Brennan."

"I mean your *first* name," Patrick said.

Well, I twern't give no first name . . ." Brennan said, stubbornly. "Ain't got one."

"Haven't got one?" Patrick said, shocked. "Everybody has a first name."

Captain Tim broke in. "Well, now Brennan, just what is yer given name? Never knew of a babe born that wasn't blessed with a Christian name. Now, c'mon, tell the boy so we can get movin'. Are ye shy? Are ye afraid of a wee child?"

Brennan puffed up like a toad poked with a stick. "I ain't afeared o' nothin' no how."

Tim was enjoying himself after the tense night steering his boat along the dark canal. "So, why don't you tell us all now?"

Brennan blustered. "Well . . . I . . . jist . . ." He paused, thinking. "It's been so long, why, I plumb fergot it!" He finished and grinned weakly.

Patrick smiled patiently and spoke as if to a very small child. "It's okay, Mr. Brennan," he said. "We promise not to laugh. Now c'mon and tell us."

"Oh, all right," the man growled. "Me given name's . . . tis . . . ."

"You can do it," Patrick urged. "It's . . . ?"

Brennan took a deep breath. "Eh, very well then. Seeing's as none of ye's about to lave a man alone! It's . . . Muireadach." He blurted. "*Mur-a-dock.* There, are ye happy? Me mam herself chose it."

All was silent for a moment. Tim's face twitched and grew red and his eyes watered, but he didn't break Patrick's promise not to laugh. Martha, unable to keep a straight face, giggled.

"That's perfect," Patrick said happily. "My dog's name is Murdock."

Brennan's shoulders sagged, all his swagger gone. "I knew it," he said, shaking his head sadly. "'Brennan,' I says to meself. 'Brennan, don't do it.'"

He went about hitching up the fresh team, muttering aloud. "Twenty long years since ye left Ireland's sod and that bother of a name behind. Ain't needed it fer this long time, then ye let a wee boy-o snake it out of ye when ye let yer guard down."

He wrestled the bit into the mule's mouth. "Hit don't matter a whit that ye'd trust 'em with yer life, when it comes to names hit's diff'ernt, I says to meself. But do I listen to meself? Oh, no-o-o-o . . . ." He bent over to check the mule's harness and his voice trailed off to a low grumble. "Now me namesake is a half-wild mongrel."

Captain Tim spoke quietly to his wife. "Martha, since we're already stopped and nothing seems to be astir, why don't ye suggest to the Browns that now would be a good time to come up, get air, stretch their limbs and visit the woods," he said.

"I don't think I'm ever gonna get used to calling 'going to the bathroom' 'visiting the woods,'" Patrick whispered to his brother.

Suddenly, before Martha could open the hatch to the cargo hold, Susan Brown burst out.

"It's the young man! He's taken on terrible sick!" she cried.

Martha picked up her long skirts, ran for the opening to the hold and hurried down the short ladder.

"He's out of his head wit' the fever," Susan explained as she followed Martha.

"Will, help Brennan tie up." Captain Tim ordered, taking the short flight of steps from the tiller to the deck in a single leap.

Susan Brown's appearance reminded Will of the real reason for their trip and he searched the towpath as far as he could see, making sure the slave catchers weren't in sight.

The sun rose higher into the sky while the *Dolley Madison* sat idle. Brennan backed the mules closer to the *Dolley,* letting the towrope drop the four feet to the bottom of the canal so that other boats could pass by without towropes getting tangled. Prudence and Mae stood patiently in the shade on the side of the towpath, their tails twitching at flies.

Will felt twitchy, too, since his earlier fear of the slave catchers had returned. Finally, Captain Tim climbed up to the tiller.

"Let's be off," he said. "We can't stay here any longer. I don't believe those bounty hunters were going to give up on us."

Patrick made a short piece of twine into a leash for Murdock. His new owner was happy with the system, but the dog had a different idea. He sat down and refused to budge, no matter how much Patrick tugged on the leash. As the boat pulled away, he hollered, "Don't worry, we'll catch up."

"Not any time soon, I reckon," Brennan said to Will. "Eh—that dog has a mind of 'is own." To Patrick he said, "You'll get along a lot better if'n you jist pick 'im up and carry 'im. Why don't you take him on deck and see if you can't find him somethin' to eat? Then he'll follow you ever'where, and ye won't need to bind 'im to ye with a rope."

"You know, I'd like to find me somethin' to eat, too," Patrick said. "I'm getting hungry."

"Tell you what," Will said. "I'll help you haul the dog onto the boat, and . . .

"His name is Murdock," Patrick said. "He'll never learn his name if you don't call him by it."

"All right then." Will said. "I'll help you get *Murdock* on deck, then go see if I can find us something for breakfast. We need to help out and not bother anybody with Adam so sick."

"What d'you think is wrong with him?" Patrick asked. "I've never been around anybody that sick."

"Neither have I," Will said. "It sounds serious, though."

"Do you think he'll die?" Patrick asked.

Alarmed, Will stopped walking for a second. He'd been so worried about the slave catchers, he hadn't had much time to think about Adam. "I don't know," he said.

"I hope he gets better soon," Patrick said.

"So do I," Will hoisted the dog and replied. "Patrick, try to remember to wash your hands and stuff before you eat."

"Martha always makes me," the boy said. "Around my neck and behind my ears, too."

"Yeah, I know, but be extra careful."

"Why? Do think we could get sick, too?" Patrick sounded a little worried.

"Well, yeah, I guess we could and they don't have medicines like we're used to," Will said. Remembering the well by the barn at home, he added, "And some of the water may not be safe to drink."

"Like the well at home . . ." Patrick stopped and glanced at Brennan to see if the man had heard what he said, but Brennan was talking to one of the mules.

"Yeah," Will said in a low voice, "like the well at home."

It took two days for the *Dolley Madison* to make the trip to Toledo. The Browns stayed below deck, only coming out late at night. After the scare Adam gave everyone, he seemed to get a little better. Martha wanted to try to find a doctor, but Adam, still very weak, insisted that with a day or so of rest he would be on the mend.

The Lake Erie docks were a busy, bustling place. Horns blared and whistles screamed. Men shouted at their teams and each other. Wagons and carts rumbled, heavily loaded with coal, wood and bulging bags of grain. Some rattled away empty, others, wheels squeaking under the burden, carried large crates of goods headed for Ohio's western frontier. Will saw that it would be easy to disappear unnoticed into the busy scene. While that could help the escaping family, it could also be a danger. No one would find two men carrying guns unusual in such a place.

Both Patrick and Will were supposed to be asleep in Martha and Tim's cabin when, under the dark cape of night, the fugitive family was escorted off the boat and into a waiting wagon. But Will had spent too many long hours worrying about discovery by the slave catchers to miss the Browns' final and possibly most dangerous part of their journey. Captain Tim said earlier in the evening that he wanted the mules and crew to rest up for a night before heading back to Junction, but that he was going to follow the wagon carrying the escaping family at a distance. He wanted to make sure they were put safely aboard the right ship for Ontario.

Will knew he would not be missed since Martha was spending the night caring for Adam. The only problem might be Brennan, who was sitting watch on deck, Captain Tim's shotgun across his lap. Thieves and robbers lived like rats among the hustle and bustle on the waterfront and often boarded boats looking for something to steal. But Brennan's two days and nights on the towpath caught up with him and he drifted off to sleep as soon as he sat down.

Patrick dropped off right away, too. Will sat up and yanked off the nightshirt he'd put on over his clothes. His heart hammered as he slipped out the cabin door and over the rail of the *Dolley Madison*. Will could see Captain Tim's tall form making his way along the street behind the wagon. Callahan turned around once to see if he was being followed and Will quickly ducked behind a cartload of barrel staves. The wagon carrying the Browns was almost to the pier when Will saw something stir under the tarp covering the wagon bed.

A corner of the cloth lifted and Ivy Brown's small face peeked out. Will wanted to wave good-bye, but he didn't dare let the child see him, so he tucked himself into the doorway of a shop that was closed for the night. He had wanted to see the Browns board the clipper with its tall masts and graceful, billowing sails. He decided to wait for Captain Tim to pass by on his way back to the *Dolley Madison*. But Brennan wasn't the only one tired out from the hard trip north. The night was warm and the breeze off the lake was soft and it wasn't long before Will slept.

"Hey! Say, you there! Get away from my shop!"

Will was startled awake by a sharp pain in his leg. Still groggy, he shaded his eyes against the bright morning sun and squinted into the face of a very cross shopkeeper.

"Go on!" The man said, giving Will another well-aimed kick. "Get out of here!"

Will leaped to his feet and looked wildly around, forgetting where he was. He stumbled away and the shopkeeper angrily fitted a key into the lock, grumbling about riff-raff and sneak thieves.

Will suddenly remembered that he had followed Captain Tim to the wharf the night before, but the captain and the wagon carrying the Browns weren't anywhere to be seen. Everything looked different in the light of day and Will wasn't sure he'd be able to find his way back to the *Dolley Madison.* He knew the Callahans wouldn't leave without him, but he didn't want to cause any problems, especially with Adam so sick.

I think we were south of here, he thought, turning slowly around. Suddenly a hand clamped down on his shoulder and he was flooded with relief.

"Captain Tim!" Will began. "I was just going to . . ." He spun around and was face to face with the older of the two slave catchers.

"Quarantine!" The older of the two spat out. "I'll wager they ain't n'buddy sick on that tub o' yourn!"

Will was speechless.

The man looked past him and shouted, "Over hyar, Virgil! Lookit! I jist trapped me a wharf rat." He shifted his grip to Will's upper arm and his meaty fist tightened. "Now, Ah reckon we ought to pay a call on the *Dolley Madison.* Visit th' ailin'. Hit's the least we kin do at a time lak this."

"But . . . but," Will found his voice, "somebody is sick! Really sick!"

"Ooh, Ah'm skeered ta death," Virgil said as he walked up. He clasped his hands together and said, in a false, high-pitched voice, "It's the diphtheria, Rafe! Whut'll we do!"

"I'm not kidding," Will protested.

Rafe jerked Will up by the arm and shook him. "You better tell me th' truth, boy! Is there diphtheria on that boat?" His eyes glittered darkly in his red face.

"No . . ." Will said, blinking back the tears that threatened to spill down his face, "but there's . . ."

"That's all Ah need t' know," the man said. "Let's go!"

"But, I'm lost," Will said. "I don't know the way back."

"Thas' quite all right," the younger of the two said pleasantly as he slid a knife out of his boot. He poked Will in the side with it. "We do."

Chapter Nineteen

Tessa and Emaline peered around the corner of the house as Eva answered the man's knock. The rusty hat was clutched in his hand and the sack lay at his feet. The girls ducked behind the wall, but the man had already seen them.

"Ah, I see the place is blessed with younguns, ma'am," he said when he saw the girls.

"Why, yes," Eva said, smiling. "We are blessed."

"Children bring life to a house, I always say," he said.

He removed the pipe from his mouth and tapped it against the heel of his boot until the cold ashes tumbled out onto the ground. He replaced the empty pipe between his lips and continued. "Now, as you can tell, I'm a tinker by trade. I go by the name of Piper O'Fahy, on account of my singing as I hike about, but I'll come to just about anything I'm called. I was wondrin' if ye might be needin' a packet of needles or perhaps a thimble?"

"Well, let's see what you have there, Mr. O'Fahy" Eva said. "I've still hot water on the stove. Would you care for a cup of tea, sir? I'm Mrs. Luke Hudson. This is our daughter Emaline and . . . and this is our niece, Tessa."

"Pleased to meet ye. That offer of tea is right kind of you, ma'am. The towpath, she gets dry and dusty this time of year. And nothin' settles the dust like a good cup of tea, I always say," he said, following Eva into the house.

While Eva prepared tea, Emaline and Tessa quietly watched as the man placed his rumpled hat under his chair, then reached into his bag and shook out a square of red cloth and spread it out on the table. Then he took paper packets of needles, pins, some thimbles and tiny sewing scissors and carefully arranged them on the cloth. He reached in again and brought out two tin cups, a small white, clay pipe like the one held between his own teeth, and a little china doll dressed in a blue satin dress and bonnet.

Emaline stared openmouthed, watching his every move. Suddenly he stopped and turned in his chair to look at her and smiled warmly. She took a step back, her eyes wide.

"Is there something special you'd be wishing for me to take out of me pack?"

Emaline shook her head, speechless for once. Her cheeks were two patches of bright pink.

"What is it, child?" The little man asked kindly. "I won't bite, ya know."

Emaline hung her head, embarrassed.

O'Fahy winked at Tessa and said, "Perhaps this young lady can tell me the wishes of the little one?"

"She . . . she doesn't really want anything," Tessa hesitated. "She thinks you're a leprechaun."

Tessa was afraid he would laugh, but he didn't. He simply nodded thoughtfully and pulled at the little beard on his chin.

"So, ye think I might be one of the little people," he said, tilting his head back and looking up at the ceiling. "Have ye ever seen one afore?"

"No, sir," Emaline whispered.

Emaline peeked up at him through her eyelashes. "But . . ." She paused.

"Go on now, speak up, say yer mind," he said kindly.

"You don't have pointy ears."

"Emaline!" Eva gasped.

Mr. O'Fahy's leathery face drew up until his eyes were mere slits. He slapped the table with both hands. His shoulders shook, the little white pipe bobbled up and down and an odd squeak escaped from around the stem.

Eva looked horrified and Emaline hid her face in her hands.

Tessa tried not to laugh out loud.

"Well, now," the tinker said, wiping his eyes, "'tis true that I come from Ireland. But, I've not got pointy ears, nor, sadder still, a pot o' gold in the bottom of me pack. But . . ."

Emaline slowly uncovered her face.

"I might have a wee bit o' magic up me sleeve," he said reaching behind Emaline's ear. He drew his hand away and slowly opened it. On his dark, lined palm laid a small gold ring.

"Oh, my," Eva said.

Tessa blinked and her mouth went dry as she stared at the dainty circlet of gold with a dark blue stone. It was shiny and polished, but it was just like the ring that tumbled to the ground on the day she was supposed to clean out the garden shed. Was it the ring that she had tucked in her pocket that day and taken to show Will? That day seemed so long ago. How long had it been? How long since that day when she and Will and Patrick had spun through the lock into the past. Days? Weeks? How long before they went back? Longing for home suddenly washed over her. Tessa heard the tinker urging Emaline to try the ring on.

"Go on, lass." he said. "It looks to be just about your size."

"Might I try it on, Mama?" Emaline asked.

"*May* I try it on," Eva said, then sighed. "Well, I suppose it won't hurt for you to just try it on," Eva said.

Emaline picked up the ring and as it passed through sunlight coming through the window, the small stone centered in the gold band glittered with blue fire. She slipped it easily onto her finger and held her hand up for her mother to admire. Tessa thought the ring looked like it was made for Emaline's small hand.

"It is lovely," Eva said. "I'm sure it's worth far more than we can afford, however. Take it off now, Emaline."

Emaline removed the piece of jewelry and handed it back to the little man.

"Where are your manners?" her mother prompted.

"Thank you, sir," Emaline said. "It's very pretty."

Eva brought two cups to the table. She placed one in front of the tinker and the other at another chair. She went to the sideboard and returned with a pot of tea and sat down.

"I surely hate to be a bother to ye, ma'am, you being so kind as to offer me a fine cup o' tea and all," Mr. O'Fahy said. "But, would ye happen to have a wee drap of sweetenin' fer me cup?"

"Oh, yes, of course," Eva said. "Tessa, would you get the honey crock, and Emaline, will you fetch a spoon for Mr. O'Fahy?" She leaned closer and lowered her voice. "I must apologize. I confess I was trying to think of a way to purchase that ring for Emaline, beings as it's her birthday next week."

"Ah, a birthday for the little one," O'Fahy said. "Now, that's a different story all together, I always say."

"I've already cut a new dress for her, from whole cloth, not one of my old dresses made over. It's the same exact blue as the glass in that ring," Eva said.

Emaline and Tessa returned to the table with a spoon and the squat honey crock. Tessa pulled out a chair and prepared to sit down. She wanted to know about the ring.

"Thank 'ee, young lasses," Mr. O'Fahy said. "Can always tell quality folk by the ways and manners of the younguns, I always say."

"Why, thank you, though I must say, there is always room for improvement," Eva said. She turned to girls, "There are some biscuits left from breakfast. Please put some on a plate for our guest. Then you girls may have one. Put some honey on them and take them outside."

After Tessa and Emaline, dragging their feet, went back outside, Mr. O'Fahy spooned some of the golden honey into his cup, stirred and thoughtfully watched the tea swirl around and around.

"The gem in that ring isn't glass, madam, it's genuine," he said. "'Tis true, I swear on me mother's grave, may she rest in peace."

"Oh!" Eva said. "Well. Then I know it's beyond our means. I do need a packet of pins, though. And perhaps that little china doll there."

"I've been waitin' until I found jest the right little girl fer this ring," O'Fahy said, turning it so the gem threw sapphire sparks. "Waitin' a mighty long time. Hiked the towpaths up and down. I'm one of the Irishmen who didn't die on the Big Ditch back in New York State. I helped to build her. Drove a mule team and scoop, I did. I fit the fever n' ague, shaking with the chills so's I couldn't keep the reins in me hands. Men collapsing all around me, being buried almost where they drapped. They don't call 'er the Irish Graveyard fer nothin', I always say. But, tisn't fittin' talk around a lady sich as yerself, Mrs. Hudson. I thought I might earn enough pay to someday be cap'n of a boat of me own. Thought me and the family would live on the canal I helped to build. But . . ."

O'Fahy paused for a moment and drank from his cup. "It twern't meant to be. Seems they grew up and scattered, like children are want to do. My wife, she died, and then I see'd I was too old to start all over, so I been traveling ever since. Ain't much left 'ceptin' this ring. Was tradin' some things with a fine old lady who lives in a big, fancy house back east Ohio. I always stop by her farm on my way through. She says the ring was hers when she was a girl and she still had it since she never had no children to pass it on to. She says that since I get out a bit in my travels, I was to look out for a special one to give it to. Told me I'd know when I saw the right little girl who the ring should belong to. And today I b'lieve I see her. I see the right spark in that little 'un of yers there."

"You don't understand, Mr. O'Fahy," Eva said, briskly. "Perhaps I didn't make myself clear. We cannot afford to spend money on such foolishness as jewelry for a child."

"I don't aim to *sell* it to ye, Mrs. Hudson." O'Fahy said, "I mean to *give* it to the child."

It was a cool, damp day. Rain had begun to fall in the night and it still dripped from the grasses and the tall oak trees surrounding the lockkeeper's house. Tessa stared out the window, the gray clouds matching her mood. She was truly homesick. She missed her mother and father. She missed Margie, and Erie's deep rumbling purr. She wanted to go back home, only she didn't know how to get there. Tessa sighed and wiped the steam that formed on the glass away with her sleeve. She wished the *Dolley Madison* would bring Will and Patrick back. Tessa was beginning to worry that she might not ever see them again, either. They had been gone for over a week.

The gloomy weather had no effect on Emaline. The next day was her birthday and she was very excited because she was allowed to have a real play party.

"Mama's going to make tea cakes with real sugar," Emaline danced past the older girl at the window. "And she says she has presents for me, Tessa! Pres-*ents!* More than one!" She skipped back and tugged on Tessa's sleeve. "Isn't that exciting? And Pa says he expects the *Dolley Madison* any time now, so Will and Patrick might come, too!"

Tessa perked up at this news. "Really, they're coming soon?"

"Prob'bly tomorrow or maybe the next day," the girl replied and she twirled around and around, watching her skirt flare until she collapsed giggling onto the floor.

"Whew! That makes me dizzy! Help me up," she asked, holding a hand out to Tessa.

Eva broke in. "That is about enough of that sort of behavior, Emaline. After all you will be another year older tomorrow, and you must begin to act like a young lady, not a circus performer. Now, you girls move the chairs aside. It is a perfect day for quilting. Maybe we can even get it finished in time for your birthday," she said to Emaline as she unrolled the long quilt frame.

Tessa wanted to groan aloud. She didn't know how to sew. A lot of her friends took 4H sewing projects to the fair, but she had never been interested. She preferred her chickens. Next year she planned on taking a beginning rabbit project. Her dad had said she could pick out a pair at the rabbit show during the fair, but so much time had passed, the fair was probably over by now. Her mood even darker than before, Tessa felt tears puddling in her eyes. She turned back toward the window and quickly wiped them away.

Eva lit a lamp and a couple of candles, and set them on the table near the quilt frame. She ran her hand lovingly over the top of the quilt.

"Come look, Emaline," she said. "Want to play the game?"

Emaline hurried over to her mother. "C'mon, Tess, 'n I'll tell you about the quilt game."

Sounds like loads of fun, Tess thought sourly.

"Here," Eva said, handing her a threaded needle and a small leather thimble. "I'm going to show you how to quilt. It is quite simple. I promise," she added, seeing the doubtful look on Tessa's face.

Chapter Twenty

Will didn't try to dodge down an alley or fade into the crowd, two ideas that raced through his mind as he trotted ahead of the slave catchers. If his pace slowed at all, the knife pricked him in the back, urging him forward. Sweat streamed down his face and soaked his shirt. After a few minutes, the canal came into view and among the boats was the *Dolley Madison,* her crisp red and blue trim shining.

"Don' be thankin' about makin' a run fer it, boy," Rafe, the older man warned. "Virgil here'll run ye down and run ye through. Don't thank he won't do it."

As the men pushed Will toward the boat, Captain Tim appeared. Seeing the look of terror on Will's face, he leaped over the rail.

"Hold up there, Cap'n," Rafe ordered. "Yer boy's safe." He elbowed Virgil and grinned. "Leastways for the time bein'."

"Will!" Martha rushed out of the cabin.

"Well, well, well, there's thet purty lil' red-haired missus of the Cap'n's," Virgil said to Rafe.

Rafe made a big show out of sweeping his hat off and bowing deeply. "Fine mornin', ain't it ma'am? I must say yer lookin' fine, too." He turned to Virgil, "She don't look ta be sufferin' from ill health, now does she?"

"Naw, sir," Rafe replied. "Naw, sir. Ah b'lieve she looks jist fine. Finer 'n frog's hair. Now why do ye reckon thet doctor put up thet quarantine sign last week? An' where is it now?"

"Gentleman," Martha said sweetly as she gathered her skirts and went to Will. "How kind of you to bring our boy back to us!" Before the men could stop her, she put her hands on Will's shoulders and smashed him close in a firm hug. "Will! You naughty boy! Your father and I were so worried! You must promise to never, never run off like that again!" She put her small hands on Will's cheeks and drawing his face to her, kissed him on the nose. It was then that he saw the fear in her eyes and felt the cold, clamminess of her shaking hands, hands that were usually steady and dry.

"Well . . . uh . . ." Rafe shuffled his feet uneasily in the face of Martha's warmth and charm.

Martha laughed merrily and with one finger, gingerly pushed the barrel of Rafe's rifle toward the ground. "Certainly you didn't have to use that much force to get a boy back in time for breakfast."

Virgil took the knifepoint out of Will's back. "Go on, boy. Mind yer ma." He said gruffly, giving him a push. "Next time heed whar yer goin' so's ye don't git lost. Our bizness is with the cap'n, anyway."

"And what business might that be?" Captain Tim asked evenly.

"Amazin' how quick a body kin recover from the diphtheria, ain't it, Rafe?" Virgil ran the tip of the knife under a filthy fingernail.

"Quicker 'n ary Ah ever seed," Rafe said.

Virgil broke in. "Seems like it were jist yesterday thet doc sez to skedaddle, thet we was in mortal danger. Yet, h'yar ye all are, fit as fiddles and right as rain. And no quarantine sign anywhars."

"Dang near a miracle, Ah'd say," Rafe said.

"I'm sure I have no idea what you lads are talking about," Tim said.

"Yep, a miracle," Rafe said. "Ya know, Virgil, jist once in my life, Ah'd like to *see* a miracle."

"That won't be possible," Tim said. He paused. "We lost him on the way here."

"Sure, sure ya did," Virgil said, then losing patience, stepped closer and spoke in a low, threatening voice.

Rafe swung around and nodded. "You lost him, or *them,* all right. You lost 'em on a fast ship t' Canady."

"We have reason to b'lieve ya'll are harborin' some propity thet don't b'long to ye and we've got the papers that gives us the right ta search fer it." He reached into his coat and pulled out a flyer like the one Will had seen in Junction.

"We're runnin' light, sir," Tim replied. "We unloaded our cargo of stove wood last night and are preparin' to head south. Search the *Dolley* if ye like." Captain Tim stepped aside and motioned the men aboard. "Ye'll not find a thing, except illness and sorrow."

Rafe stepped closer and glared up at the captain, then started toward the *Dolley*.

Suddenly Patrick staggered around the corner of the cabin, clutching his throat and making terrible gagging and retching sounds. "Mama," he managed to choke out before falling to the deck, where he rolled back and forth, coughing and spitting. Murdock ran around the boy barking.

"Rafe!" Virgil said nervously. "Ah ain't never had the diphtheria, but I seen somebody die from it and it weren't a very good way to go . . ." He looked worriedly at Patrick.

"Not my baby!" Martha ran to Patrick and gathering him in her arms, carried him to the cabin. Murdock pranced behind, tail wagging.

Tim said, "Now, if you'll be on your way. As you can see I must go for a doctor. Perhaps it's only the grippe, but I wouldn't want you fellers to take any risk.

With a stream of curses that Will had never heard before, Rafe stomped off the *Dolley Madison* and down the wooden dock. Virgil loped along behind like a faithful hound.

Captain Tim bent down and picked up the crumpled flyer the slave catcher had thrown down in disgust. Brennan stepped out from behind the cabin, grinning.

Adam seemed better for a short time. On the return trip, the fever that raged through his body broke, leaving behind a pinkish rash. The *Dolley Madison* was almost to Providence when Adam left his narrow bunk and shakily made his way on deck.

"Well!" Tim said when he spied the thin young man leaning wearily against the stable cabin. "You are a sight for sore eyes, boy-o!"

Adam waved weakly at the captain and coughed.

"Martha!" the captain called. "Look here!"

Martha came out of the stern cabin, a dish cloth in her hands.

Tim said, "Look who's back among us. I reckon it won't be long until he's up and at it again."

Martha hurried over to Adam. "Are you sure you feel up to stirring about already? You haven't taken any food or drink for days. You must be terrible weak."

Adam attempted a laugh that ended in a cough and he bent slightly, clutching one arm around his stomach, holding onto the cabin wall with the other. His large eyes, usually a dark, shining brown, were dull and muddy in a face that was chalky gray under its tan. His lips were dry and cracked.

"I ain't never been a shirker. Got to get back to work sometime," he said. "Besides, the fever's gone away."

Martha laid the back of her hand on his forehead. "True. You're cool—almost cold, for such a warm morning as this. Those spots that are coming out all over are a troublesome thing, though. You will not go back to work until the captain says you may," she said firmly. "And I'll be the one telling him when you may. If truth be told, I don't mind admitting you had all of us mighty worried there for a while."

Adam smiled thinly. "Don't fret about me." With his back to the cabin wall, he slid to the deck of the boat, his long legs stretching straight out in front.

"There now, you just sit in the sun and . . ." Martha bent over, peering closely at the young man and gently prodded his shoulder. "Adam?"

At her touch, his head fell limply to his chest.

"Tim!" Martha cried. "It's Adam!"

Brennan halted the mules and the boat slowed. Tim scooped up the thin young crewman and carried him back to his bunk before the *Dolley Madison* came completely to a stop.

Brennan called to Patrick. "C'mere, boy!"

Patrick climbed over the side of the boat and jumped onto the towpath, with Murdock scampering right behind. The dog had been Patrick's shadow from the moment the boy laid claim to the half-grown pup.

"So ye think ye kin handle this team?" Brennan growled.

Patrick nodded silently.

"Hey? Well, speak up, then!"

"Yessir!" Patrick said.

"I'm goin' ta fetch a doc," Brennan said, handing over the reins. "Keep me girls cool and unhitch 'em if the cap'n says to."

Brennan nodded at Will. "You fetch fer Miz Callahan if she needs anything and be quick about it."

The tough old driver yanked the brim of his battered, sweat-stained hat down and shuffled off at a fast clip, taking the tow-path in the direction of the small village of Providence.

Will listened as the Callahans followed the doctor up onto the deck.

"Are you sure, Doctor?" Martha asked, her eyes filling with tears.

The physician that Brennan had dragged back to the boat tilted his head slightly in her direction and peered over the top of tiny spectacles balanced on the end of a nose that was bumpy and crisscrossed with bluish veins.

"Am I sure?" He took a deep breath and his stomach, already straining the buttons on his waistcoat, swelled to the point where Will feared they would give up and shoot off in all directions.

"My dear woman, I know the symptoms of typhoid fever well enough to make a certain diagnosis when I see them—the fever, the rash . . . I've seen it before and I'll see countless more cases of disease among these . . . these . . ." With a theatrical wave of his arm, he plucked a perfumed handkerchief from his pocket and held it delicately to his wrinkled nose. " . . . these canal workers and the human rubble that follows after them. They are the ones who bring these fevers and plagues to decent folk."

Tim Callahan's eyes narrowed to two slits.

"That smell to which ye seem so averse is the odor of human sweat, sir," he said, his voice dry and cutting as a January wind. "Perhaps it's not familiar to yer refined nose because it's the smell of hard work and honest labor."

The doctor blinked and took a step back. "Well! I . . . I . . ." His plump lips tightened like a purse string and his double chin quivered.

"Now, Tim," Martha said, taking her husband's arm, "the doctor did come all the way out here to see Adam."

"Well, it weren't because he had a burnin' desire to help one in need," Brennan broke in. "He's jist travelin' through, but he was the only one I come upon. He needed a wee bit of persuadin' afore he decided 'twas in his best interest to come along with me."

The mule driver made the motion of raising a glass to his lips. Then he tilted his head back and from between his few teeth, squirted a thin, brown stream of tobacco juice over the side of the boat, just missing the doctor's shoulder. A look of horror passed over the doctor's face and Martha's hand flew to her mouth.

"Pardon me, Missus," Brennan said to Martha as he wiped his chin on his sleeve, "I fergot meself, it's just that this here . . ."

The doctor nervously cleared his throat, took a careful step away from the scowling Irishman and turned toward Captain Tim. "There is the matter of my payment. Plus an extra charge for my trouble, you know," he said, holding out a pale, puffy hand. "And none of that paper canal money. It's often worthless."

The captain drew a small sack from his pocket, held it up and shook it gently. At the clink of coins, the doctor's round face lit up greedily.

"Well, now, that's better," he said. "I see we understand each other."

"Oh, aye," The captain said as he carefully selected a gold coin. "I understand you, that's fer sure. Here, if ye ain't too good to take a canaler's money, sire. Cap'n Tim Callahan always pays his due."

He held out the money and just as the doctor reached for it, the captain flipped the coin with his thumb. It spun high into the air before falling into the canal with a musical *ploop*. The doctor, who followed the graceful arc of the shiny disc until it was swallowed up by the murky green water, snatched up his small leather satchel with a grunt. He turned on his heel, marched over the short gangplank and off the *Dolley Madison.*

"Why I believe the good physician forgot his money," Tim said with mock concern.

Brennan laughed.

"Oh, Tim," his wife said.

When the doctor was a safe distance away, he turned around and shouted.

"You had best pray to the Almighty above that boy there is the only one who comes down with the fever!" He started off, then stopped and turned around again, mopping his forehead with his handkerchief.

"By the way, I forgot to mention, it's not likely he'll last through the night."

At the doctor's words, Martha rushed back down the steps into the hold to be with Adam. Seconds later, she called out.

"Tim! Hurry!"

"Boy!" Brennan's voice made Will jump.

"Best come away from there, boy," the man said in a softer tone.

The captain reappeared and motioned for Brennan. Brennan also disappeared below deck, but was back in a short time.

"Eh, Will," Brennan said, then stopped to rub his eyes. "Got a speck in me eye. Anyway, the Missus needs ye to . . . to go into town fer some supplies."

"What kind of supplies? Is Adam all right?" Will asked, puzzled. Martha had never asked him to do her shopping before.

"And yer to take little Patrick with you," Brennan said, ignoring Will's question. "Get some . . . some thread . . . and needles."

"Thread? Needles?" Will asked. "Doesn't she need some sort of medicine or something for Adam?"

A look of pain passed over the man's face. "Nay, nay . . ." He was beginning to look panicky.

He dug in his shirt and pulled out a handful of coins. He grabbed Will's hand and slapped the money into it. "Git on yer way now!"

"But, I . . ." Will protested.

"Go on now, git!" Brennan barked.

"Okay! Okay! We're going!" Will said. "C'mon, Patrick!"

Will and Patrick, with Murdock panting happily alongside, started toward Providence at a trot.

"Will!" Brennan called.

Will turned around.

"Uh, git yerself and the boy there some candy," Brennan said gruffly.

"Did Brennan really say we could get candy?" Patrick asked. He was walking with Will, stopping every once in while to toss a stick for Murdock, then running to catch up.

For the first time in days, Will wasn't worried about slave catchers. Still his heart beat hard and fast against his ribcage as he hurried Patrick along the towpath. Was Adam really dying? Was the fever catching? Will was scared for Patrick. And scared for himself.

"Did he?" Patrick asked.

"Did who what?" Will asked. He'd been so lost in his thoughts, he hadn't been listening to Patrick's cheerful chatter. "Oh, candy. Yeah, he said to get some candy."

"Gee!" Patrick said.

As he and Patrick hiked, Will's thoughts turned back to the day he'd bought candy for everyone at the dusty little store in Junction. That was the day he first saw the slave catchers who where so bent on getting their money, they almost ran Tessa and Emaline down. It was later that night he'd discovered the Browns in the loft of the Hudson's house.

"I sure showed those slave catchers, didn't I?" Patrick asked.

Will turned and grinned at his brother. "Dude, you sure did. That was some fast thinking."

"Not to mention some great acting," Patrick added.

"Did Brennan give you the idea to roll around like that?" Will asked.

"Well, he did give me the idea that if I acted really, really sick it might scare those slave chaser guys. But, he didn't tell me how. I thought it all up myself." Patrick said proudly.

Will tousled Patrick's hair. "That was some great acting because it worked."

Murdock yapped happily at Patrick and the boy picked up another stick and threw it.

"What's typhoid fever?" Patrick asked when he caught up with Will again.

"That's what Adam has, I guess," Will said.

"Yeah, I heard that dumb doctor," Patrick said. "I think Adam's gonna die and that's why they sent us into town. To get us out of there."

Will thought there was a very real chance that his brother was right and a wave of homesickness mixed with fear surged through him. Things had been getting more and more dangerous and he wanted to return to the safety of home. He wasn't sure how much longer he could protect Patrick from the rough life on the canal. He didn't know how to get home, though. He needed time to think, but they were almost there. Providence lay directly ahead.

Providence, like Junction, had grown quickly. Its saloons, mills, stores and houses had sprung up along the canal like toadstools after a rain. Although a huge fire had nearly destroyed the town in 1846, and many of its citizens had died during a cholera epidemic the year before, Providence once again thrived with business and canal traffic. As the boys approached, they came upon a line of boats waiting for their turn to go through a lock. A fife and fiddle played a lively Irish tune and two canalers jigged to the music, while others stood about talking or squatting in small circles, tossing dice. About halfway down the row of gently bobbing boats, a loud voice rose over the general bustle.

"I'll show you what fer, ye dang hinny! Now gi'up there!"

A sharp crack followed and a mule squealed. Patrick, a few paces behind Will, stopped in mid-step.

"Hey . . ." Patrick said, and instead of turning and following his brother on into the village, he headed toward the boats.

"Patrick!" Will called. "C'mon back here!"

Patrick, with Murdock at his heels, either chose not to hear, or made up his mind to keep going despite his brother's warning.

"Patrick!" Will called again. It was too late. Patrick's red head was already bobbing through the crowd gathered around the source of the uproar. Will tried to follow, but his brother was quick and soon out of sight.

"I'll teach ya not to bite the hand that feeds ya!" the voice yelled again.

Crack! Another mule scream ripped through the air and Patrick broke into a run, Murdock yapping at his feet. His bare feet smacking the hard packed towpath, Patrick darted through groups of canalers and around mule teams.

A tall man, so thin his tattered clothing hung like rags on a scarecrow, swung a piece of board and hit a mule in the ribs with another loud "thwack!" The mule, its yellow teeth bared, squalled. It reared and bucked, back legs kicking. One flying hoof caught the man in the shin. Howling and letting loose a string of colorful curses, he dropped the board, grabbed his leg and hopped around on the other foot.

A small crowd of boatmen, restless and bored with their long wait at the lock, had wandered over, eager for entertainment.

"I'd step in," one said, "but them mules of Bony Smith's are meaner than he is."

"Don't I know it," another man said. "A feller from down Loramie way tried to stop ol' Bony from beatin' his mules. The only thing he got for his trouble was a bite on the arm that mortified. Laid him up for nigh onto three months. Had to hire his boat out just to keep food on the table. Dang near lost that arm."

"Who bit him?" Someone in the crowd asked, "the mule or Bony?"

The canalers roared with laughter.

Patrick wiggled his way unnoticed through the knot of men until he reached the frightened mule.

"Hey! You stop that!" Patrick shouted as Bony Smith picked the board up and prepared to deliver another blow. Before the man could swing it again, Patrick jumped up and grabbed the man's upraised arm with both hands.

Will's stomach lurched when he heard Murdock barking and the roar of men's voices. He squeezed between two burly canalers and dodged around another, yet he still couldn't see his brother.

"What the . . ." The man lifted his arm higher into the air with the boy dangling from it. "Git off'n me, ya little rat!"

The board rattled to the ground as the man shook his arm, as if trying to rid himself of an annoying insect. But the little boy clung tighter than a tick behind a dog's ear.

Laughter rippled through the crowd as Bony, resembling a dancing coat rack, flapped around trying to shake the child loose.

At this, the fur on Murdock's back stood straight up and his top lip curled back over his teeth. A low warning growl came from deep in his throat. The dog gave one loud *gr-r-r-ouf,* then with teeth bared, sprang at the seat of Bony Smith's baggy britches.

Chapter Twenty-One

Later, Tessa had to agree that Eva was right. Quilting, once she got the hang of it and in spite of many painful needle pricks, *was* fun.

Eva had sewn many small pieces of fabric together into squares called blocks. When the blocks were put together they formed a pattern she called "Ohio Star." The top, made of all the blocks put together, was placed over a soft, warm center of cotton, called the batting. The bottom layer of plain cloth was the back. The quilt fit together like a sandwich. All three layers were stitched together by sewing around each individual piece of fabric that made up the double-pointed stars.

"It's sort of like a puzzle," Tessa observed to Eva. "Trying to decide where to go next with the needle."

"Why, yes, I believe you're right," Eva said.

Tessa stopped to admire her work. When compared to the tiny, straight stitches that followed the quick movement of Eva's needle, Tessa was surprised to see the crooked path her large, clumsy ones made.

"Oh! Mine are terrible!" Tessa said.

"They aren't terrible," Eva said. "They are your first, and they will only get better"

"But they'll spoil Emaline's quilt," Tessa said.

"No, they won't," Emaline said, leaving her chair and coming to Tessa's side. "When I'm all grown up and a mother, I'll cover my children with this quilt and every time I'll say: 'Children, my friend Tessa made those stitches.'"

Emaline climbed back onto her chair and patted the quilt top. "Let's play the quilt game, Mama."

"You start," Eva said.

Emaline got up on her knees and leaned over the quilt frame. "See this patch with the tiny little flowers? They're from my dress I wore two years ago," she said. "I won't have any from last year's dress 'cause you gave it to . . . to . . ." She stopped.

"To Ivy Brown for her trip to Canada," her mother finished. Emaline looked relieved. "Yes."

"I had a few tiny scraps left from when I made that dress and they are in here. So, in a way, you will be able to remember her, too. Without saying a word." Eva smiled. "See if you can find them."

Emaline studied the quilt for a minute. "There! There's one! And here is the dress Mama got married in, Tess. She wore it until she cut it down for a dress for me. It's the one with blue stripes over there by you." She pointed in Tessa's direction. "See it?"

Tessa searched, then found the dark blue scrap. It was part of one of the large stars centered in the middle of a block. "Yes," she said, "and there's one over there, too."

"See, you can play the quilt game, too," Emaline said. "Sometimes I go around and count all the pieces I can find of the same pattern."

"If we want to finish in time for tomorrow, perhaps we should have a little less chattering and counting and a little more stitching," Eva said kindly as she walked around to the side of the quilt frame where Tessa was working. "Let's see how you are coming along." Then she stepped back and smiled down at Tessa. "I can see improvement already. You'll make a quilter, yet."

"Not like Rosemary," Emaline snickered.

"Oh, Emaline, you should be ashamed," Eva said.

"Who is Rosemary?" Tessa asked.

"Poor Rosemary lives on the next lock over," Eva explained. "She's just a young thing, newly married to the lockkeeper there. She comes to all the quilting bees and works so hard. But . . ." She trailed off.

"But all the ladies take her stitches out the minute she leaves because they're simply awful," Emaline finished.

"Don't say awful. It's such slangy talk," Eva corrected her daughter. "It's true, though."

"Mama *never* takes anyone's stitching out, though," Emaline said. "She says a quilt is the sum of all who work on it, and it's the loving thoughts that go into it that are the most important."

"Well, that's good," Tessa said, eyeing her work. She plunged the needle into the quilt again and stabbed her finger.

"Ouch!" She yelped and yanked her hand out from under the quilt and stuck her finger in her mouth.

Emaline laughed. "I forgot to tell you about that part!"

"Oh, look! I've ruined it!" Tessa cried. A large crimson spot of blood had dropped onto a piece of the rosebud material.

"No, no, you haven't," Eva said. She poured water onto a rag, wrung it out and dabbed at the spot. "See, most of it has lifted."

"I'm sorry," Tessa said.

"Every quilter has done the same thing," Eva said kindly. "Why, I still do. It happened just the other day. I was working on a dark piece, and it can't be seen, that's all."

"I'll just tell my children, 'See that spot, children . . .' " Emaline said.

"My friend Tessa did that," Tessa joined in.

Eva, Emaline and Tessa all laughed.

"Ho! What's all this?" Luke Hudson stepped into the house. When he opened the door, sunshine streamed into the room.

"Why, I declare!" Eva exclaimed. We've been so busy, I didn't even notice the sun had come out!"

"Maybe it will be nice for my birthday, after all," Emaline said. "I wish Patrick and Will could be here."

"I was expecting them before this," Luke said. "They might have had a chance to make a short haul somewhere along the way. Never can tell during the busy season."

"I'll fix us some supper and we can go back to quilting after we redd up for the night, girls. At least as long as the light lasts."

"Why don't you two go out and collect the eggs? We'll have some for our supper and save the rest to take into town and trade," Eva said.

"Aw, Mama, I don't want eggs again," Emaline said.

"Is that any way to talk to your mother?" Luke asked.

"I didn't mean to talk sassy, Papa," Emaline said, looking down. "I'm just not very hungry, I guess."

"It's all this talk about cakes and birthdays," Eva said briskly. "Go on now, do as you're told."

Tessa took up the egg basket and headed out the door. "Are you coming Emaline? You're so much better getting eggs out from under that one old broody hen. She always pecks me."

"I'm coming," Emaline said, dragging her feet. She stopped at the door and turned around. "I sure do wisht it was tomorrow now, though. I'll never be able to go to sleep tonight. I'm too excited."

Luke and Eva laughed.

"You do your chores and that will help tire you out," Luke said. "Birthdays have a way of coming even when you think they never will."

"Well, I'm glad of that!" Emaline said and skipped out the door.

"Oh, Luke," Eva said as she watched the little girl head down the path toward the hen house, "I do believe I may be even more excited than she is!"

"Let me see the ring again," Luke said.

Eva reached into her apron pocket, pulled out a knotted handkerchief and untied it.

"You know that funny little O'Fahy fella stopped and talked quite a spell with me before he headed north on foot," Luke said, taking the ring from Eva's palm and holding it to the light. "D'you suppose what he said about that old lady wanting a little girl to have this is true?"

"I had no reason to doubt him," Eva said. "He seemed an honest sort."

"I've heard talk of him from different boats coming through the lock, and none of it's ever been bad," Luke said, handing the jewelry back to his wife. "In fact, a lot of the canalers think he brings good luck. It will give her a story to tell her own children some day."

"I just hope she understands and appreciates it," Eva said. "She is still such a baby yet. And I hope it doesn't spoil her for next year's birthday—a doll, a new dress *and a ring*. And I think I may get this quilt finished up, too. I believe we are spoiling her, Luke."

"Well, Eva," Luke said quietly. "I don't know that we are . . . after all, she's the only one of our children that lived."

Sadness washed over Eva's face, then she shook herself and looked up at her husband. "But she *did* live and tomorrow will be a special day."

Luke said, "Too bad the boys won't be here, unless the *Dolly* shows before then. Haven't heard of anyone catching sight of her, though."

The next morning dawned as bright and sunny as the day before had been cloudy and gray. Tessa awakened to the chirp of birds and the strong smell of coffee from downstairs. She stretched, rolled over, then smiled when she saw the Ohio Star quilt folded neatly at the foot of Emaline's bed. Emaline was still asleep. Her fine hair had worked out of its bedtime braids and spread in silvery-blond wisps across the pillowslip. Her cheeks were pink and she mumbled something in her sleep. Tessa carefully picked a feather out of her pillow got out of bed. She stood over the sleeping girl and tickled her nose with the tip of the goose feather. Emaline brushed at the end of her nose. Tessa did it again. This time, even though her eyes remained closed, a grin grew across Emaline's face and she grabbed Tessa's wrist. Her eyes popped open.

"Caught ya!"

Tessa laughed. "Happy birthday!"

"Happy *ninth* birthday," Emaline corrected as she sat up. She spotted the quilt, complete and spread across the bed.

"My quilt! It's finished!" She exclaimed as she scooped up the quilt and hugged it. "It's a good birthday already!"

Emaline and Tessa were disappointed that the *Dolley Madison* hadn't arrived by the time the breakfast dishes were cleared away, but they held onto the hope that she might appear at any moment. Each time the high, clear notes of a horn sounded alerting a boat's approach, they raced to the lock, only to be disappointed.

"Oh, well," Emaline said. "It's still my birthday and mama is making a cake. We can save Will and Patrick a piece."

At supper, Emaline jittered in her chair and pushed the food on her plate around with her spoon.

"You're not eating much of that fried chicken and biscuits your mother made special just for you," Luke said. "Fried chicken, in the middle of the week, yet. Never heard of such stuff and nonsense," he said, reaching for another drumstick.

"Why, look at that," Eva said, "only one bite of biscuit gone, Emaline." She looked closely at her daughter. "You feel all right? You look a little flushed."

"I guess I just want some of that cake," Emaline said.

"And maybe presents?" Tessa teased as she buttered her second biscuit. "Since it's your birthday, I'll help Aunt Eva with the dishes and you can go play after supper."

When Tessa carried the pan of dirty dishwater out to dump on the garden, Emaline was sitting on the swing, spinning in circles and watching the pattern her toes made in the dust.

"Your mother says for you to come in now and see your presents," Tessa called.

"You don't have to call me twice!" Emaline said. She stood up and staggered, catching herself from falling by grabbing the rope. "Whoo! Now I'm dizzy! Kind of made me feel sick, too."

When she got to where Tessa stood waiting for her, Tessa noticed a dark smudge under the girl's nose.

"Here, you've got some dirt or something on your face," she said, taking from her pocket the handkerchief Eva insisted girls should never be without. "Let me wipe it off for you."

When Tessa drew the cloth back from Emaline's face, it was smeared with blood.

"Well, look at that. You've got a nosebleed."

Emaline was impressed. "I do? How about that! Let's go show Mama."

But when the girls entered the house, Emaline forgot about her nose because Eva had the table spread with plates from her wedding china. The teapot, out along with a small cake sprinkled with real sugar, were in the center. Three packages, one large and two small, were wrapped in brown paper and tied up with Emaline's Sunday hair ribbons.

"Oh," Emaline breathed. "Oh, it's all so pretty and lovely!"

She unwrapped the package that held the dark blue dress that Eva had worked on each night after the girls had gone to bed, every stitch sewn by hand in the wavering light of a kerosene lamp.

"I can't wait until the preacher comes around and we can go to meeting so's I can wear it. Then I can use my good dress for everyday."

Emaline held the dress up to her shoulders and whirled around. "Oh! That makes me dizzy!" She put a hand to her head and fell into a chair.

"We'll have to start a new quilt, Mama," she said, "with the scraps from this dress."

Eva said, "I have other things to do right now, with everything in the garden getting ripe and those Early Harvest apples ready to be cut up and dried. But, come this winter, we'll get out the scrap bag and begin another quilt. You may choose the pattern."

"Let Tessa choose," Emaline said as she smoothed the new dress over her lap. "It's her turn to have a quilt."

"Why yes," Eva said, "so it is. Didn't you say your birthday is in March, Tessa?"

"March 7th," Tessa answered.

"I love my Ohio Star, but you could pick Flower Basket," Emaline suggested, "or Double Wedding Ring, they're pretty ones. Say, maybe we could even have a quilting bee!"

"We'll see," Eva said. "Perhaps after the canal closes for the winter."

Luke set his cup down. "That's probably about the earliest you'd want to do something that like," he said. "Doctor Ayres came through today. Looked terrible, too. Hasn't had any sleep for three days now. Says he has a full-blown epidemic on his hands. Says that's why he was traveling on the canal, so's he could sleep between towns. He can't trust that new horse of his to go home on his own like old Patriot used to."

"What kind of epidemic?" Eva asked as she filled his empty cup from the teapot.

"Well," Luke hesitated and. "He said most of the cases are typhoid fever, although he's seen some fever and ague, too."

"Typhoid fever!" Eva said. "Then it was in Defiance after all."

"Ayres says that the worst of it is centered around Junction," Luke said. "Doc thinks it might be the town well, but seeing as it seems to have started with the canalers in the boarding houses, there's a committee forming, to try and run all the strangers out of town. There's a couple of characters they won't have to bother with, though. And they aren't canalers."

Eva looked puzzled.

"Those two bounty hunters." Luke said.

"The slave catchers?" Eva asked.

"The same," Luke replied. "They went all the way to Toledo and didn't have any luck. On the way back to Junction, I'm happy to report, one of them come down with the typhoid. His brother took off and left him and it wasn't a day before he was gone."

"Luke!" Eva said. "You shouldn't speak so of . . . of the ill . . ."

"By gone you mean . . ." Tessa said.

Emaline stared, owl-eyed, taking in every word.

"Yep! He died and no one there to take care of the bod . . ." Luke trailed off when Eva scowled at him over their daughter's head. He cleared his throat and quickly changed the subject.

"Three presents! And a cake! he said. "What little girl around here has been good enough for a three-present birthday?"

Emaline giggled with delight, her eyes shining, "It's really four, Papa, counting my quilt."

"There's a story behind the tiny packet there." Eva smiled at her daughter as Emaline unfolded the paper from around the ring.

"The ring!" Emaline cried. She slipped it on her finger. "Oh, I do feel all grown up now!"

"It's said the best things come in small packages," Eva said, looking at her daughter. "I believe that just may be true."

Chapter Twenty-Two

It was hard to tell how many years Bony Smith had been around. He was as gray as his old boat the *Minerva* and his skeletal mule, Scratch. The small, once tidy craft had been neatly painted white with red shutters and yellow trim. Now grayed by years of weather and neglect, the bright colors had peeled and faded, leaving as a reminder of better times, a faint pink stain on the few shutters that hadn't fallen to pieces. Time had not been any kinder to Bony Smith than he was to his mules. His head was bald except for a few thin, greasy strands of hair that hung over his shoulders and down his back. Ancient dirt lined the wrinkles and creases in his leathery face. Most of his teeth had rotted away, or fed up with the pain of toothache, he'd yanked them out himself. Now his chin and long nose almost met.

Another gaunt mule stood in the stable on deck, up to his knees in soiled straw. The animal's eyes were cloudy and its muzzle was frosty with age. The stable's roof sagged and had rotted away in places, leaving large holes that let in the hot sun or the cold rain. Most of the siding, from which Bony had broken off the board he was using on his mule, was broken or missing. A crusty bucket hung on the wall, but it was as empty of cooling water as the feed trough was lacking oats and hay.

"Should'a knowed it was Bony Smith behind the ruckus," one of the canalers said as he puffed thoughtfully on a clay pipe with a curved stem. "You can smell him and the *Minerva* long before she hoves into sight. I'd like to see that lad best the old miser."

"Bony, he's powerful tight with his money. Never spends a cent if he don't have to," another man said. "He believes in getting every last penny's worth out of anything, be it beast or boat."

"Aye, that's true. He's powerful close with his coin," a short, stocky man in a battered beaver top hat agreed.

"His coin and ever'body else's," another canaler chuckled. "It doesn't matter to ol' Bony."

"I've heard," the top-hatted man said, lowering his voice and looking over both shoulders. "I've heard tell that somewhere on the *Minerva* he's hidden away a sack of gold so big and heavy that one of these days, it'll bust right through that rotten hulk and sink straight to the bottom."

"Bony Smith's got every intention of taking his fortune with him, wherever he ends up," another canaler said.

"I'll warrant it'll be a durn sight further down than the bottom of the Miami and Erie," a young, broad shouldered teamster said. "But say, I believe that little lad's had about enough. What say we go help him out, boys?"

Patrick was still hanging on, but his grip was weakening, while Murdock, swinging from the seat of Smith's ragged britches, showed no sign of letting go. Luckily for Smith, the dog's teeth had closed around a mouthful of the man's pants and nothing else. The thin yellow dog swung back and forth like the pendulum on a clock. With each swing, Murdock had managed to work Bony's pants down a little farther. The lower the pants went, the louder the laughter was from the crowd of onlookers. When the dog finally let go, Bony Smith's pants were down around his knees.

Finally, by prying each of the boy's fingers free one at a time, Bony Smith was able to loosen Patrick's hands. Patrick dropped to the hard ground bottom first, raising a small cloud of dust. He scrambled to his feet and ran to the mule that was hungrily tearing at a small clump of grass. Murdock let go, and neatly avoiding a kick from Bony's Smith's boot, ran to Patrick.

"Don't you hit this mule again!" Patrick shouted, climbing up onto the animal's back. He leaned over, wrapped one arm around the thin neck, and twined his other hand into the coarse mane.

"Why you little . . ." Bony Smith picked up the board, raised it above his head and started toward Patrick. Murdock barked wildly and dashed in and around the mule's hooves.

At this point, the canalers surged toward the man, toppled him into the dirt and someone pulled the board out of his grasp.

But it was too late.

The mule, seeing his owner coming toward him with an object that had caused him pain so many times before, reared up, his eyes rolling back until the whites showed. Patrick hung on as the mule backed away in blind terror.

When he finally managed to push his way through the wall of men, Will saw Patrick on the wildly careening mule. Some of the teamsters were trying to circle the animal as it backed toward the canal, but too many years of abuse at the hands of one man had created within the animal a hatred of all men and it was not about to let them catch him.

"Patrick!" Will cried.

Patrick looked up for just a second before the mule, crazed with fear and confusion, took a final step back, lost its footing on the embankment, flipped over, and plunged into the water with the boy still holding fast. Murdock leaped into the water after them.

The crowd froze as the mule and Patrick, then the dog, disappeared under the water. Neither Patrick nor the dog was to be seen when the mule resurfaced. The animal floundered, legs slashing the water into foam as it tried to find solid footing on the steep slope.

"Patrick! Patrick!" Will screamed from the bank. "Somebody help him!"

He dashed to the water's edge, and paying no attention to the pounding hooves of the mule, jumped toward the spot he had seen the surprised face of his little brother disappear as the water of the Miami and Erie washed over him. But just as his feet left the towpath, something jerked him back. He struggled to get free, but the strong, young teamster held him by his shirttail.

"Hold up there, young feller," the man said.

"Let me go! My brother! In there! Have to get him out!" Will cried, squirming to get free.

"Calm down now, boy. Look-a-there," the teamster said, jerking his chin in the direction of the *Minerva*.

Will looked and there, bobbing like a like a small, redheaded cork, was Patrick. He swam toward the edge of the canal where a boatman tossed him a line. Patrick grabbed the line and was lifted out of the water as easily as a stringer of fish.

At the same time, one of the other canalers fashioned rope into a loop and threw it neatly over the mule's head. The young canaler let go of Will and jumped into the canal in spite of the danger of the thrashing mule. But, having had no rest or much food, the animal tired quickly, and quieted at the approach of the kind young teamster. He talked softly to the animal. After guiding it to a level spot, and with the help of the men pulling steadily on the rope, the mule was able to climb the rest of the way out.

Later Will didn't recall running to his brother. He just remembered how good it felt to wrap his arms around Patrick's sturdy little body.

"Patrick! I thought . . . I thought . . ." Will didn't continue.

"You thought I drownded?" Patrick asked cheerfully.

"Yes," Will choked. "Are you okay?"

"I'm okay." Patrick said, pushing his streaming hair back from his face.

"Are you hurt anywhere?" Will asked, his hands moving down the boy's muddy arms.

"I'm . . . I'm . . . not hurt anywhere."

Will noticed a large rip below the right knee of Patrick's overalls from which a flap of torn fabric dangled. Beneath, a trickle of blood mixed with canal water ran down his leg.

"What about that?" he asked, bending down to get a better look.

Patrick jerked his leg back. "It's just a little scratch. Geez, will you ever quit treating me like a baby?"

"Okay! Okay!" Will laughed and stood up. Then he remembered what had sent Patrick into the canal in the first place. His eyes narrowed. "What were you doing anyway? I can't take my eyes off you for a second! You could have been killed and then Mom and Dad would kill me if . . . if . . . they ever found out . . . if we . . ." His voice trailed off.

"If we ever get back, you mean." Patrick said.

"Yeah," Will said.

Patrick turned, searching for the mule that he had ridden into the canal. "Is that mule okay? How did it get out?"

"Wait a minute," Will said, grabbing the straps of Patrick's overalls and raising him slightly off the ground. "Wait a minute! You still haven't told me what you were up to!"

Patrick wiggled helplessly, his feet pedaling in midair. "Put me down and I'll tell you."

Will lowered his brother until his feet touched earth again.

Anger flashed in Patrick's green eyes. "That man, he was so mean to that poor mule."

"What man?" Will asked.

Patrick said. "Oh, Will! Can't we buy 'im?"

"Buy who? The mule or the man?" Will laughed.

"It's not funny!" Patrick said. "He was going to *beat* him with a *board!* Maybe beat him to *death!*"

"Who was going to beat who with a board?" Will asked, then sniffed and wrinkled his nose. "Whew! Patrick is that you?"

The boy sniffed at his dripping arm, then looked up as a shadow fell over him. Patrick's eyes traveled up and up until they stopped at a point high overhead and he gulped noisily. "It's not me, Will. It's him!"

Will spun around and found himself face to face with Bony Smith, whose colorless lips parted in a twisted smile, revealing a few stubby brown teeth.

Chapter Twenty-Three

"Hello, there young sir," Bony said to Will with a gust of breath that smelled of onions and decay. "Might ye be the one responsible fer this young rascal?" He pointed a knobby finger with a thick crescent of dirt under the nail at Patrick.

"I . . . I'm not afraid of you," Patrick said, his chin jutting out. "And . . . you stink!"

"Patrick!" Will hissed. "For once in your life *shut up!*"

"This here yer brother?" Smith asked Patrick.

The boy nodded.

"He speaks sense, that's fer sure," the man said to Patrick, bending over and looking him up and down with squinty eyes. "Seems to me yer a mite too big fer yer breeches."

The man stood up and turned his gaunt face to Will. "I've a mind to report both o' you'ns to the marshal or maybe even the canal authorities. There's laws against meddling with a man's property like he done."

"Yeah, well there are laws against . . ." Will stopped because he wasn't exactly sure what had happened. "Against what you did to my brother," he finished lamely. "He could have been killed."

"He coulda killed my mule," Smith growled.

"*You* could have killed your mule!" Patrick shouted.

"Patrick!" Will glared at his brother.

"Well, he could have . . ." Patrick trailed off.

Bony ignored the outburst. "How some ever . . ." His voice became smooth and oily as he rubbed the palms of his hands together, making a sound like two pieces of sandpaper. "There's ways o' takin' care o' things without gittin' the law involved or havin' to sign a raft o' papers and such."

"Yeah?" Will said warily. "How?"

"If ye was to, well, let's say, *make amends* fer all the fuss yer little brother caused . . ."

"You mean *pay* you?" Will said.

"Well, now, if ye want to put it in *them* kind o' words . . . Somehow it jist don't seem as friendly like." Smith shook his head sadly back and forth and sighed, sending another foul breeze into Will's face.

Will turned away and swallowed down the urge to gag. It gave him a second to think.

"All right, all right," he said, turning back, this time breathing through his mouth. "I guess you're right."

Patrick's mouth dropped open. "Will! What are you . . ."

Will shot Patrick a glare and making his voice as deep as he could, said to him, "Well, say now, young lad, I wager we've had just about enough out o' you fer one day!"

Patrick's eyes widened at his brother.

"Well, now," Bony said, "I see we's in agreement."

"Yes-sir!" Will said, sticking his hand in his pocket and making a big show of jingling Brennan's coins. "Yessir! Never let it be said that I'm a man who don't pay his claim. Now then, my friend, just what do you reckon it will take to settle our little . . . uh . . . dispute?"

Patrick took a deep breath and was about to protest when Will grabbed him by the shoulders, and squeezing tightly, turned him around. "Jist simmer down there lad."

Bony's eyes gleamed at the sound of the money and he licked his lips. "Let's see now," he said, tilting his head to the side and scratching at a two or three-week growth of beard. He closed his eyes, happily trying to decide how much he could cheat the boys out of.

The moment Bony took his eyes off the boys, Will yanked Patrick's overalls and yelled, "Run!"

The boys took off and it was a second before Smith, lost in a pleasant little daydream about the lovely coins he was soon going to add to his stash, realized the source of his new wealth was hot-footing it down the towpath. Will and Patrick had placed a size-able distance between themselves and Bony before the man raised the alarm.

"Thieves! Stop them thieves! Don't let 'em git away!" he shouted. "I've been robbed!"

"Omigosh, omigosh, omigosh!" Will panted. "Can't you go any faster?"

Patrick, still dripping from the canal, tucked his head down and his thin arms and legs pumped faster, but then he stopped suddenly. "Murdock! We forgot Murdock!"

"Pickpockets! They got my money!" Smith yelled.

"Can't—go—back—now!" Will puffed. "C'mon!"

Suddenly, a large man stepped in front of the boys and held out his well-muscled arms. First Will, then Patrick slammed into the broad chest. Clutching each boy by the neck of their shirts, he knelt down, looked at Will and then Patrick. It was the young teamster who had stopped Will, then jumped in to help Bony Smith's mule out of the canal.

"Say, now, what's this all about?" he asked, not unkindly. "Things sure have been hoppin' since you two blew into town. And Ol' Bony sure seems to have a gripe with someone. Would that happen to be you two?"

Will was too out of breath to answer and Patrick dangled, panting, from the man's grasp.

"We . . . we didn't steal anything!" Will gasped. "Honest!"

"Honest!" Patrick wheezed.

"He was trying to steal from us!" Will said.

"He says you have his money," the man said.

"I have money," Will admitted. "But it's not his!"

"Where did you get it?"

"Someone gave it to me."

"Oh, I see," the young man said, raising sandy eyebrows.

"Brennan gave it to him!" Patrick said.

"Brennan, you say?" the man asked. "Brennan, driver on the *Dolley Madison*?

Patrick nodded eagerly. "Yep, Muireadach Brennan, driver on the Dolley Madison."

The man let go of the boys and stood up. "Muireadach? Brennan's name is Muireadach?" He tipped his head back and laughed. "Muireadach! Oh, I've got that old skinner now!"

"I was supposed to buy some stuff. That's why Brennan gave me the money. But then Patrick got into trouble trying to help that bony guy's mule and . . ."

"I think I can just about figure out the rest," the young driver said.

"Now do you believe us?" Will asked.

The man smiled. "I suppose I do at that. But why are you in such a bestir to get back?"

"It's Adam," Will said. "He's really sick."

"Adam? The young bowsman?"

"Yeah," Patrick said. "The doctor said it was some kind of fever. He called it, um . . . tife . . . tife . . ."

"Typhoid fever?" the man asked.

"That's it," Patrick said. "Typhoid fever."

The driver's smile melted and he stood up. "Come then. I'll take you back. Let's get moving before Ol' Bony catches up."

"But I have to get Murdock!" Patrick was near tears. "Will, we can't just leave him behind! He's just a puppy."

"Son," the man said, "I think we best be on our way back to your boat. Ol' Bony will cause an uproar and it'll take a long time to get it all untangled."

"Murdock!" Patrick wailed. "I have to find Murdock! He mighta drownded!"

The man, who, like Patrick, was still wet from his dip in the canal, pulled out a soggy handkerchief, wrung it out and handed it to the boy. "Don't know as that will do you much good . . . what's your name?"

"Patrick," the boy sniffed.

"My name's Samuel, but most people just call me Muley, Muley Sam."

"I'm Will and I'm getting out of here!" Will said, half-jokingly as he started off for the *Dolley Madison*.

Muley chuckled as he scooped Patrick up and followed. "Can't say as I blame you," he said.

"Murdock!" Patrick said sadly, staring over Muley Sam's shoulder as they left the village behind.

"I'll try and find your dog when I get back," Muley said to Patrick. "Dogs have a way of turning up just when you think you'll never see them again."

He turned to Will. "Ol' Bony's breath could unravel your socks, eh?"

"You said it, Muley," Will said, smiling for what felt like the first time in days. He didn't know it was the last time he would smile for many more, for by the time that he, Muley Sam and Patrick got to the *Dolley Madison*, Adam was dead.

Chapter Twenty-Four

Three days after Emaline's birthday, the *Dolley Madison* finally floated into sight. Tessa sat on a low stump watching as the boat grew bigger as it drew near. She rested her folded arms on her knees and laid down her head. The *Dolley* didn't look any different than the other times Tessa had waited for her to arrive at the lock, yet everything couldn't be more changed than it was now.

Emaline was sick. Very sick. In the middle of the night after her birthday party, Tessa had been awakened by Emaline's moaning.

"Emaline?" Tessa said. "Did you have a nightmare?"

"No," the child sobbed. "It hurts."

"What hurts?"

Emaline didn't answer. Although Tessa couldn't see the girl in the dark, she could hear her thrashing around in her bed.

"Mama, mama!" Emaline cried weakly.

Tessa hurried to the loft opening and called Eva and Luke. "Aunt Eva! Uncle Luke! Come quick! Something's wrong with Emaline!"

Eva, long hair braided for the night, climbed up to the loft, her white nightgown caught up with the same hand that held a candle. Luke was still in the kitchen lighting a lantern.

Eva knelt by her daughter's bed, holding the candle high. "Emaline? What is it, honey?"

"It hurts," Emaline whispered.

Eva smoothed the damp hair away from Emaline's forehead. "Oh, you're burning up. Where does it hurt?"

Emaline turned her face to her mother. "My . . . head . . . my tummy," she whispered.

Eva peered closely at her daughter, bringing the candle closer. "What is that . . . ?" She touched Emaline's face and brought her hand to the candle. It was smeared with a thick, sticky liquid. "Blood!"

Emaline, moaning, rolled over and was violently ill on the floor.

Eva stood up abruptly, staring down at her daughter. "Luke!" She cried. "Luke! Get the doctor!"

When the *Dolley* finally reached the lock, Brennan trudged by with his mules, with his eyes on the ground and no gap-toothed grin for Tessa. She was surprised, but when Will was the only one to jump out and tie the boat to the snubbing posts, Tessa felt a chill of worry. She hurried up to help her cousin wrap the heavy rope snugly around one of the posts.

"Where's Adam?" She asked.

Will didn't answer.

"Did he take a job on another boat?" Tessa looked at the *Dolley's* strangely empty deck. "Hey, where's Patrick?"

"Sick."

"Sick?" Tessa asked, her stomach twisting in fear. "They're both sick?"

Will, squatting by the snubbing post, stopped winding the rope, stared at his feet for a moment, then stood slowly and faced Tessa. His eyes were red with dark circles under them.

"Adam isn't sick," he said. "Anymore."

"Is he . . . ?" Tessa asked.

Will nodded.

But . . . wha . . . how?" Tessa stuttered. "Was it an accident?"

"No," Will said. "Typhoid fever."

"I never heard of it . . . before now," Tessa said, thinking of Emaline.

"Well, it doesn't matter if you've heard of it or not, does it?" Will snapped. "He's still dead, isn't he?"

Tessa grabbed her cousin's hand. "Patrick!" The words choked her. "He's . . . ?"

Will shook his head, "No, but he's sick!"

"So is Emaline!"

"Is it . . . ?" Will said.

"Typhoid," Tessa said. "Is that what's wrong with Patrick?"

"I don't know," Will said, swiping at his nose with his sleeve. "They think so. He has a really high fever."

"Where is he? I want to see him." Tessa said. Her voice shook.

"He's in Tim and Martha's cabin. But, they won't even let *me* see him! They're afraid I'll get it, too. But, Tess," Will looked miserable, "I can hear him calling for me. He needs me and I can't get to him!"

"Will," Tessa said. "We have all got to get out of here!"

"I know, I know," he said. "But, how?"

The *Dolley* docked at Lock 32 and the day crept slowly into night. Tessa tried to help by doing dishes, keeping the bucket full of fresh water from the well, taking care of the chickens and mainly by staying out of the way. Emaline had been moved to the Hudson's room and Eva sat by the bed, bathing Emaline's fevered body with rags dipped in cool well water.

Will helped Brennan by forking soiled straw out of the mules' stalls and putting in fresh bedding. Brennan let both mule teams rest and graze under the deep shade of the tall oak trees. Luke had saddled his horse and been gone, searching for the doctor since well before dawn. It was dusk when he finally returned with Dr. Ayres.

The doctor's face, always solemn, looked more drawn than usual after seeing Emaline. From their post by the lock, Tessa and Will quietly followed the doctor onto the *Dolley* and listened intently as low voices came through the cabin wall. The words were muffled and Tessa could only make out a few, so she quietly slipped up and pressed her ear to the door. She heard Dr. Ayres say "not sure" and "must wait" and "time will tell."

"What in the name of Zeus are you two up to?" a harsh voice rumbled.

Tessa jumped with a little "eep!"

"Brennan!" Will said in a loud whisper. "We . . . we were just trying to hear how Patrick is."

"Ah-ha, I see that. Well, then," Brennan said, producing a small, round wooden box with both ends cut out, "let's go about this the right way. Move over."

He squeezed between Tessa and Will, placed the box on the wall and pressed his ear to it.

"Can you hear anything?" Tessa whispered.

"Shhhh," Brennan hissed, placing his finger to his lips. "I can't hear anything a'tall now."

"Well now," another voice said from behind the three crouched against the cabin wall, "there's a good reason for that."

Tessa and Will whirled around and Brennan quickly tucked his homemade earphone back into his pocket. Eyes wide and mouths open Tessa and Brennan stood guiltily with their backs to the cabin.

"Captain Tim!" Brennan said. "I was just tellin' the kids here . . ."

Martha folded her arms, raised an eyebrow, and for the first time in many days a smile tugged at the doctor's lips.

"Aw right, aw right, you caught us," Brennan admitted, shoving both hands in his pockets and staring at his well-worn boots. "We jes' wanted to know how the little boy-o is doin'."

"How is he?" Will stepped up to the doctor.

"The truth is, son, I don't know for certain," Dr. Ayres said. "The child certainly has the fever and the headache . . ."

"No nosebleed?" Will asked.

"Not all cases of enteric fever—typhoid—present with that symptom," Dr. Ayres said. "In fact, many don't. Patrick doesn't have a rash, but one could present itself at any time. It's puzzling."

"Can I see him? I want to see him. He needs me," Will said firmly.

"I don't think that is wise," the doctor said.

Martha, seeing the disappointment, then the flush of anger on Will's face, put her hand on his arm. "Come, Will, please try to understand. We don't want to lose . . ." Her voice cracked and her chin trembled.

Tim cleared his throat. "We need all the help we can get right now, boy. Won't do to have you down sick, too." He spoke sternly, but in the last rays of the setting sun, Tessa saw the concern in his eyes.

"He's sleeping now and that is the best thing for him at this time—and for you, too, Mrs. Callahan. I insist that you get some rest before you are stricken," Dr. Ayres said. "I'll be back tomorrow."

Tessa opened her eyes. Something, a sound, had awakened her. *Tick!*

There it was again.

Tick! The sound was coming from the single window on the far end of the loft. Tessa rolled out of bed, trying to keep the ropes that supported the feather mattress from squeaking. As she tiptoed toward the window, she noticed the half moon had deepened to gold and was riding low in the sky. It was almost morning.

Tick! Something was hitting the glass! Pressing her nose against the glass she looked down. It took a moment for her eyes to adjust, but when they did, she could see Will standing outside the lockkeeper's house, his arm back, aiming at the window.

Tessa waved her arms back and forth and Will must have seen the white of her nightgown in the dim moonlight, for he stopped throwing pebbles. Stepping as carefully and quietly as she could, Tessa went soundlessly down the sturdy wooden steps and glided across the kitchen to the door. She could see lamplight spilling from underneath the crack under the door to the Hudson's bedroom and the murmur of voices as Eva and Luke tended to the ailing Emaline.

Will was waiting for her when Tessa slipped outside.

"Hurry!" he whispered, tugging on her arm. He pulled her away from the house and toward the lock where the *Dolley* was moored. When they were away from the house he said, "Now's our chance. They're all asleep. Come on, we're going to go see Patrick."

"Where is everyone?" Tessa whispered.

"Cap and Brennan are down in the hold sleeping," Will said. "Martha rested first and took the second watch, only she fell back asleep."

When Tessa followed Will into the cabin, she saw that he was right. Martha, exhausted by the days and nights she spent nursing Adam and now Patrick, had fallen asleep. Her head was cradled in her arms on the table, a bag of knitting had slipped unnoticed to the floor. A stub of a candle still flickered, but melted wax had formed a puddle at its base that had spread out over the table before hardening.

Moving over to Callahan's tiny sleeping chamber, Will gently shook Patrick's shoulder.

The boy woke and blinked sleepily at his brother. "Will!"

"Shh!" Tessa and Will said together, casting anxious glances in Martha's direction.

Tessa felt Patrick's forehead, it was very hot and his hair stuck damply to it. Will sat at the foot of the bed and his brother jerked in pain.

"What's wrong, Patrick?" Tessa asked. "Does your stomach hurt?"

"No."

"Head?"

"Just a little."

"Then what . . . ?"

The boy pointed toward his leg.

"Your leg?" Tessa asked, puzzled. She quickly pulled the sheet away and lifted Patrick's long flannel gown up.

Patrick whimpered and said, "The mule kicked me when we fell in the canal and now it's mortified."

"Mortified?" Tessa asked as she leaned closer to Patrick's lower leg. Even in the dim light, it was noticeably red and swollen and a faint odor came from it. She stood up.

I think mortified means infected," she said to Will.

"I can't see it very well, but I can tell it's infected," she said. "You can smell it. Here, smell it . . ."

"No, thanks, Will said hastily. "Patrick, didn't the doctor see this?" Will said.

"No, that's when you guys bumped against the wall and they all went out to see what was going on," Patrick said.

"Well, why in the world didn't you tell him about it?" Tessa asked. "They think you have typhoid fever!

"'Cause it's mortified and they'll cut it off!" Patrick began to cry softly.

"Where did you hear that?" Will said.

"Brennan. I heard him telling the Captain about somebody he knew got a cut on his leg and he said it mortified and they cut it off and he died anywa-a-a-ay . . ."

Tessa clamped her hand over the sobbing boy's mouth and looked across the cabin where Martha, tired from nursing the sick boy, was miraculously still asleep.

"Listen to me!" Tessa hissed. "You can't cry now. You have to be the big brave guy I know you are!"

Patrick, eyes wide in the darkness, nodded.

Martha stirred and Will motioned to Tessa that they needed to leave.

"Don't go!" Patrick held onto Will's sleeve.

"Don't worry, we'll think of something," Will said.

Tessa hugged the boy and whispered, "Now go to sleep."

"Will?" Patrick said sleepily.

Will turned around. "What?"

"Have you seen Murdock?"

"I'm still looking." Will lied.

"Okay." Patrick whispered sadly. "G'night."

Once back on shore, Tessa said to Will, "It's almost light. I have to get back before they notice I'm gone. Don't you think we ought to tell somebody about that leg? Maybe there's something they can do for it. You know Patrick's fever probably means the infection has spread past his leg. What are we going to do? He *could* lose that leg." *Or even worse,* Tessa thought. "I wish we were home," she said aloud. "He'd be fixed up in no time with antibiotics."

"I know, I know," Will said. "That is exactly why we aren't going to tell anyone about that leg. Didn't you ever read anything about the Civil War? They cut arms and legs off just about the minute anybody gets a scratch. We *can't* tell them."

"I really, really want to go home," Tessa said. "I'm scared."

"Me, too," Will said. "I was awake all night trying to figure out how to get back." *If something happens to Patrick,* he thought, *I will never, ever forgive myself for letting him down when he really needed me.*

"I want to see Mom and Dad. They're probably worried sick," Tessa said. "We have to go home. But how do we get out of here?"

"I don't know." Will said. "Go back to bed. We'll both think about it and talk later today."

"We'd better come up with something soon," Tessa said. "Patrick . . ."

"Patrick's life depends on it, I know," Will said. "I'm his older brother. He trusts me to take care of him. I have to figure out a way."

The two separated and had walked a short distance when Tessa thought of something.

"Hey?" she called softly.

"Yeah?"

"Who is Murdock?"

"He's Patrick's dog," Will said with a sigh. "It's a long story. I'll tell you later."

But, it would be a long while later before Tessa heard the story of Murdock.

Chapter Twenty-Five

Tessa made it up to the loft and had just climbed back into bed when she heard the Hudsons' bedroom door open and the sound of Luke's boots as he ran across the floor and jerked open the outer door.

"Hurry!" She heard Eva cry as the door slammed. "Please, hurry!"

Tessa turned her face into her pillow and prayed.

It was all over so quickly, Tessa thought. She was sitting under the oak trees, tossing kernels of corn to the chickens that had followed her after letting them out of their coop.

She reached in the apron pocket and pulled out the ring with the blue stone—Emaline's ring. Eva and Luke had given it to her two days before, the day of Emaline's funeral. It fit her pinkie finger, but it felt awkward and wrong. The ring didn't belong to her. It was Emaline's. It matched her blue eyes and her new blue dress . . . the dress in which she'd been buried. Tessa couldn't bear to think of those lively, sparkling eyes closed forever. She couldn't stand the thought of Emaline's dancing feet forever still, buried in the cemetery on the other side of the woods.

First we were having a birthday party, she thought, and then . . . tears, never far away the past few days, pooled in her swollen eyes and spilled over, leaving wet stars on the creamy white of her apron.

Tessa didn't want to think about it any more, but pictures kept flashing through her mind like a broken video—Eva leaning on Luke, her face a pale mask of shock; Luke's eyes dark with pain as the plain wooden box that Luke had made, covered by Emaline's birthday quilt, was carried to the *Dolley Madison;* the little cemetery in a clearing in the woods; the opening in the ground beside three tiny markers all carved with the same words—*Infant Hudson.* Emaline was buried beside her baby brothers and sister. The worst memory was Eva falling, to the mound of fresh earth, clutching handfuls of it to her face, screaming over and over, "No! No! No!"

Tessa had only been to funerals for old people—her grand-parents, an elderly neighbor—never someone close to her own age. Then the casket, or coffin, as everyone called it, was at the front of a big room in the funeral home, surrounded by flowers. When Emaline died, it was very different.

Word got out that the Hudson child was ill and neighbor women came to help. They cooked and cleaned, carried out the soiled bed sheets and boiled them in a pot of water that hung over a fire in the yard. When it grew dark, they gathered around the lantern on the table and quietly waited, mending or needlework in their laps. Tessa wished Martha could be there for Eva, but she was so busy with Patrick, she could only get away for a few minutes at a time.

Tessa felt like a shadow. She helped where she was needed and stayed out of the way when she wasn't. She took care of the chickens without being asked to, feeding them, letting them out in the morning, closing up the henhouse at night, carefully collecting eggs, even from the crabby old broody hens that pecked her hands when she reached into the nest boxes.

That was where she was when she overheard Luke talking to Dr. Ayres.

"But, Eva and I drink the same water Emaline does," Luke said. "Why aren't we sick? Why isn't Tessa sick?"

"Perhaps Emaline drank from the well in Junction," the doctor said. "I have so many cases there. It's no longer just the canalers that are falling ill."

Tessa started. An egg slipped from her hand and cracked onto the floor as the scene in Junction played out in her mind. She saw again the candy, Emaline drinking deeply from the tin cup at the well, then handing her the cup just as the racing horses' hooves pounded toward them. In a strange way, the slave catchers had saved Tessa's life by knocking the cup of water, teeming with typhoid bacteria, from her hand and sending it flying.

"Seems like the other kids would have had a drink at the same time as our girl," Luke said.

"You know children," Dr. Ayres said, "never really know what they've been about."

Emaline died very differently from the way she lived. She slipped so quietly away that Dr. Ayres had to press an ear to her chest for a long time before he sadly nodded at Eva. Tessa expected Emaline's mother to cry or scream, but she simply sat, holding both of her daughter's hands as they grew cold. Luke fell to his knees and gathered up the limp little body and buried his face in the shining, wheat-colored hair. Martha, tears sliding down her face, gently urged Tessa toward the bed. Unlike Eva, Tessa cried, cried in great gulping sobs, to see her sweet friend white and still as the small china doll that sprawled on the bed by Emaline's pillow.

Brennan carried in a large board of freshly sawed oak and laid it on the bed, bringing into the room the clean smell of wood. Luke and Dr. Ayres lifted Emaline's body onto the board, then they left. The women brought a bowl of warm water and some soft rags to Eva. The last act of love she could give her daughter, she slowly washed Emaline's body and dressed her in her new dress and right down to her pantalets, stockings and shoes. Then she brushed Emaline's hair, coaxing each strand around her finger until it curled. Then she went to her dresser drawer and brought out a new satin ribbon and tied it in a bow around the blonde hair. When she was finished, she leaned over and kissed the tiny pink scar on Emaline's forehead, yet Eva still shed no tears.

People, the ones that weren't down with fever, came from all around and stayed up all night with the Hudson's as they sat by their daughter, lying on the board that rested on two chairs. Candles were lit and stayed lit until dawn. Tessa sat wishing for Will, but he refused to leave his post by the *Dolley Madison's* cabin door, waiting and watching for Patrick. Old hymns were sung and people prayed. The night dragged on and Tessa's head began wobble as she fought sleep. She was so tired. Her head ached and her eyes burned from crying. Soon her chin dropped to her chest and she slept. She awoke at daylight, lying in her clothes on top of the featherbed in the loft, covered with a quilt. It was the day of Emaline's funeral.

Tessa sighed and shook her head, trying to forget that day. One of the black and white hens picked at something by her foot. It was one of Emaline's little acorn teacups. Tessa threw the rest of the grain on the ground and while the chickens busily pecked it up, she sank onto the tea party stump, laid her head down on her arms and let the tears come again.

Chapter Twenty-Six

"Do you really think it'll work?" Tessa asked Will.

"It has to work," Will said.

"I mean it sounds so simple," Tessa said. "We should have tried it before."

"*We* didn't think of it before," Will snapped, and then his voice softened. "We didn't have to before. There's no time left. Now we have to."

Tessa nodded, her heart thumping. Will was right. There was no time to lose. If they didn't do something soon, Patrick was going to die. When he had been allowed up, Martha had noticed him limping and discovered the half-moon shaped wound on his leg. Dr. Ayres had been called back in. Despite all of his of "poultices and plasters" and using leeches to drain away the "bad blood," the infection had gotten worse. Patrick's fever rose and his leg was angry red and swollen to almost twice its size, causing him to thrash about in pain.

"Dr. Ayres just left," Will said. "I heard him tell the captain and Martha that if it wasn't any better tomorrow . . ." He stopped and looked away.

"So, what you're saying is we can't be here tomorrow," Tessa said.

"Yeah."

That night Tessa waited for Will, wide awake and jumping at every little sound. Her eyes had begun to grow heavy when finally she heard the *tick* of a pebble against the window glass. Although it was very late, a lamp still burned downstairs.

Already their plan was in trouble, she thought. The Hudsons should have been asleep, but ever since Emaline had died, Eva slept very little. Tessa hated to leave right when the Hudsons were so heartbroken over the loss of their only child—but Patrick's life depended on getting back home. She had no choice.

Tessa slipped quietly over to the window and waved her arms to stop Will from tossing another stone. He motioned for her to open the window. Tessa pushed it, but the wood was sticky from the humid summer air. She shoved hard, and with a loud squeak, it popped open. She stiffened, her heart hammering in her chest. No one started up the steps, so the noise must have blended in with the loud chorus of night insects outside.

While Tessa wrestled with the window, Will ran back and forth from the woodpile, hauling logs and stumps and stacking them under the window. The lockkeeper's house was small, so the distance to the ground was not far for a second story. By crawling out the window and hanging by her hands, Tessa's toes would almost reach the top log. She slipped her nightgown over her head and stood fully dressed except for her boots. She had been afraid they would make too much noise. Both hands on the window ledge, she peered out at Will who was pointing to his wrist, then at the sky. The stars had dimmed and the night had lost its velvety blackness. It was almost dawn. They had to hurry.

Taking a deep breath, Tessa climbed out and let herself down, stretching her toes as far as she could.

"Let go!" Will whispered. "I'll catch you!"

With a silent prayer Tessa opened her fingers and dropped. Her right foot knocked against a log and it tumbled to the ground with a soft thud. But Will kept his promise and caught Tessa, breaking her fall. They landed in a heap, unhurt. They froze for a moment, holding their breath for fear that someone inside might have heard the log when it fell. Luckily, the brick walls of the lockkeeper's house not only kept it well insulated from heat and cold, but also from sound.

The two scuttled around the corner and headed for the lock.

Then Tessa tapped Will and held up a finger.

"I'll be right back," she whispered.

She went to the window that was glowing soft gold with lamplight, and peeked inside. Eva Hudson was in the rocker, Emaline's quilt spread over her lap. She was sewing, her head bent low over her work. The needle threw sparks of reflected lamplight as it flew rapidly in and out as the woman attached a dark border to the already completed quilt. In a small basket at the woman's feet were scraps of the dark blue cloth used to make Emaline's birthday dress.

As Tessa watched, she felt a sadness so heavy that her breath caught in her throat. "Will, I don't think I can leave them like this . . ." she whispered.

He gently tugged her away from the window. "You have to, Tess," he said.

Tessa turned away, and then stopped.

"*What now?*" Will said.

Going to the corner of the house, Tessa counted silently: five bricks up, ten bricks over. She pried open Emaline's secret hiding place, then pulled the tiny gold ring with the sapphire stone off her finger, set it inside and replaced the brick.

When they were well away from the house, Will whispered, "Why did you do that? Didn't the Hudsons want you to have it?"

"It doesn't belong to me." Tessa swallowed hard. "It belongs here . . . with them. Well, c'mon. We'd better put this great plan of yours into action. How are we going to get Patrick out of the cabin without anyone hearing us?"

"We're not," Will said. "If my plan works, we won't have to."

The *Dolley Madison* was moored on the south end of the lock, near the wastewater weir. By the spillway, she was out of the main part of the canal and wouldn't hold up the other boats coming through. Luke Hudson had left the lock fit so that the first boat headed north in the morning would be able to float in without delay. As Will unwrapped the rope that held the *Dolley Madison* moored to a tree beside the towpath, one of the mules in the stall cabin snorted. He stopped for a second, and when no further sound came from the stable, continued. At the same time, Tessa, on deck, uncoiled the other rope. Will climbed aboard and padded silently to the other side of the boat, climbed over the side and silently slid into the canal. He swam the few feet to the embankment and crawled out. When he stood up, Tessa tossed him the coil of rope. She picked up her rope, walked down the short gangplank leading to the towpath and waited for Will's signal.

Will waved his arms at Tessa. She waved back. They were ready.

Will's mouth was so dry, his tongue stuck to his teeth. What if it didn't work? What would happen to Patrick? To Tessa? To him? Although they'd only been on the canal a short time, he felt like a different person than the day they rowed into Lock 32. Patrick had changed, too. He wasn't nearly as annoying as he used to be. In fact . . . Will *liked* Patrick. He had always loved him because they were brothers, but now he actually enjoyed having him around. And now his brother was sick, sick and in danger of dying. He had to help him!

"Will!" Tessa hissed.

Well, Will thought, if I'm ever going help Patrick, now is the time.

Tessa and Will each pulled as hard as they could on their ropes, but nothing happened. It was going to be harder than he thought. The *Dolley's* stern wasn't built to go backwards. It was broad and flat, not like the prow that was shaped to cut through the water. Will motioned to Tessa again. The second time Will pulled until his eyes bulged, his feet slipping and sliding as he leaned forward. Tessa dug her bare heels into the towpath and used the strength in her lower legs.

Sweat was running into Will's eyes and the rough rope had rubbed the palms of his hands raw by the time the *Dolley Madison* finally began to move. Once in motion, the boat floated easily between the sandstone walls of the lock, and Will and Tessa had to scramble and pull in the opposite direction to keep the *Dolley's* stern from crashing into the closed gates on the north end of the lock.

Will motioned to Tessa again and they met at the thick gates.

"Here goes," he said quietly. "I hope it works. I just thought if we came in through the lock, maybe we can go back that way. Since we've gone through it a lot of times the right way and nothing happened, I thought maybe if we go through *backwards* . . ."

In answer, Tessa began to turn the big iron handle that opened the little doors—the wickets—that emptied the water out of the lock back into the canal. But she could barely move it. Will grabbed hold and together they cranked it open, then quickly moved to the other gate and did the same. It was only a few minutes until the water in the lock was level with the canal on the north side of the doors.

Then, like he had done so many times before, Will placed the flat of his hands on a sweep—one of the large beams that stuck out to the side of each gate. Tessa did the same on the other, and as they pushed, the doors silently opened. Even though the *Dolley* was backward, she began to float into the lock. Tessa ran and jumped on deck. Will gave the rope a final good tug to hurry the boat along, and then joined Tessa. His feet made a hollow thump when they hit the wooden planks of the deck, but it didn't matter now if they were discovered. Tessa grabbed his hand and they stood together while the *Dolley Madison* began to spin . . .

Patrick sat up. Perhaps it was the pain in his leg or a sound, but he was wide-awake. Even with his fever and aching leg, he felt something was different. *Murdock!* Maybe he'd come back. Muley Sam had scoured Providence for the dog with no luck. After Adam's death and burial near the little village, the *Dolley Madison* had returned to Junction and everyone else had forgotten the skinny, half-grown pup—everyone except me, Patrick thought. But maybe Murdock had managed to catch up after all!

Patrick crawled out of the little bed the Callahans had made for him on the floor. Taking the broom from its spot beside the door and using it as a cane, he stood up and made his way out onto the deck.

At first it was too dark to see anything, but he heard the creak of the great lock gates as they opened. He felt the boat move forward as it passed out of the lock, only it was going backwards!

Suddenly the cabin door burst open and Captain Tim, holding a lantern high overhead, ran out, practically tripping over Patrick.

"Hey!" he shouted. "Hey! What's going on?"

The mules reared and squealed and Brennan rushed up from the hold.

"We're movin'!"

The sky began to revolve around Patrick. The broom clacked to the deck as it fell from his hands. Already dizzy and weak from his fever, his knees only wobbled briefly before buckling. As he went down, everything began to spin faster and faster—the deck and the sky swirling together with the light from the captain's lantern in the center, an eye in a hurricane. Then complete darkness fell. And silence.

"Patrick!" The voices were high and tinny and came from very far away.

"Patrick! Wake up!"

"I don't think he hears us." It was Tessa.

A hand shook him. "Patrick!" It was Will.

Patrick moaned.

"There! He's coming around now." Tessa again.

Patrick's eyes refused to open.

"Patrick!"

"Tessa, I don't feel so good . . . dizzy . . ." He moaned.

"He's awake now," Will said, relief in his voice.

Patrick opened his eyes and squinted as the white summer sun beat down on his face. He smelled the mossy scent of water and heard the dry rustle of reeds and the thump of an oar. He was in the johnboat.

"Hey," Will said kindly, "it's about time you woke up. It's almost suppertime."

Will kept rowing and Tessa climbed over and knelt by Patrick. He sat up.

"Tessa!" Patrick said, trying to jerk his leg out of her hands as she slid his sock down. "What are you doing?"

Patrick's leg was smooth and whole, not swollen and purple with infection! She looked more closely. A few inches above his ankle lay a tiny horseshoe shaped scar. Tessa looked at Will, relief flooding her face, then gently put her little cousin's leg down and pulled his sock back up.

"I thought I saw a tick crawl under your sock," Tessa said.

"Did you get 'im?" Patrick asked.

"Yep," Tessa said, making a pretend flicking motion with her fingers. She gasped when she saw the gold band with a blue stone on her little finger.

"What?" Will asked.

Before Tessa could answer, a warm, wriggling body leaped into the johnboat and onto Patrick, slathering his face with a warm, wet tongue. Barley's deep woof joined Margie's excited whimpering as he splashed into the canal.

"Murdock!" Patrick cried.

"Murdock?" Tessa laughed. "That's Margie!

"And Barley!" Will added.

Chapter Twenty-Seven

That was last summer and now it was September and they were back in school. Tessa sighed as the big yellow bus slowed, turned and rumbled into the school parking lot. In a single body, even though they had been told to remain seated, the entire sixth grade noisily stood and began crowding into the aisle. They piled up, waiting for the bus driver to push the lever that opened the double doors.

"Aren't 'cha comin,' Tess?" Cassie said as she slung her backpack over her shoulder.

"Go ahead. I have to ask Will a homework question," Tessa said, remaining in her seat.

"Okay." Cassie said, already shuffling toward the front of the bus. "I'll probably call ya tonight."

"Okay," Tessa said absently. "See ya."

Will sat patiently as the rest of the class poured down the bus steps and out into the freedom of the rainy afternoon.

"Well?"

He looked up to see Tess looking down at him. "Are you going to sit here all day? I think I'll go home. Come over after chores, okay?"

"Yeah," was all he said.

By the time Tessa finished feeding her chickens and collecting eggs, the rain had come to an end and the sky was growing lighter in the west. She looked out the barn door when she heard Margie yapping happily. Will, Barley loping behind, was turning his bike into the driveway. Tessa was surprised to see Patrick happily pedaling beside his brother. She quickly checked out Will's face, because when he had to let his little brother tag along, he usually wore a sour expression. But this time he was smiling at Patrick and even laughed at something the younger boy said.

Margie raced toward the drive, barking a happy welcome to the boys and Barley. Tessa followed.

"Hi," Tessa said to Will with a puzzled look in Patrick's direction. "I thought you hated it when he tags along."

"He didn't tag. I asked him to come along," Will said. "Anyway this is about that quilt . . . on the field trip today. That's why you wanted me to come over, isn't it?" he asked.

"Well . . ." Tessa took a deep breath. "Yeah. It is, sort of. Remember the day we took the *Miami Mist...*"

"**Marvelous** *Miami Mist...*" Patrick broke in.

"**Marvelous** *Miami Mist,*" Tessa corrected herself. "Anyway, Will . . . that . . . that night . . . we . . ." she trailed off and looked pointedly at Patrick.

"The night we came back?" Patrick piped up.

Tessa looked at Will, her eyes widening

"It's all right. You can say it in front of him," Will said. "He knows."

Patrick looked from his brother to Tessa, grinning.

Tessa held her hand out. On her pinkie finger was the ring with the blue stone.

"Emaline's ring! But . . . I thought you put it behind that brick the night we . . ." Will said.

"I know," Tessa said. "You watched me hide it in the bricks. Anyway, when we were back in your boat, I noticed this on my finger," Tessa said.

"It came back with you? Why didn't you say anything?" Will asked.

"I guess I forgot about when Margie jumped into the boat," Tessa said.

"So, what are you going to do with it?" Will asked.

"I think I know, but there's something I want to show you first," Tessa said. "C'mon. I'll get my bike."

The three, with Tessa in the lead and Barley and Margie trotting behind, pedaled down the road about a half mile and then turned down a narrow, grassy lane. The grass and weeds, still wet from the day's rain, slapped at their legs and soaked their jeans to the knees. The lane widened and ended in a very small, very old cemetery.

"We've brought bag lunches here a million times," Will said. "What's the big deal?"

"Don't you remember?" Tessa asked. "Look, she said pulling the long strands of a Virginia creeper vine back from a weathered stone. "You can't read it because it's too worn down, but if you trace it with your finger, you can make out some of the words."

Will knelt on the damp ground and slowly ran his index finger up and down and around the lines and curves of the carved letters and numbers. He spelled aloud as he went.

"Can't make out the date, but the year is 1850," he said. "The name is . . . E-M . . ."

"It's Emaline!" Tessa couldn't wait for him to finish. "I know this is her stone. It has to be. And look, there are the three other ones. Her baby brothers and sister! I remember these markers from Emaline's funeral."

Will stood up and stared silently at the tiny stones that were almost lost in the weeds.

"I can't find anything with Luke or Eva on it, though," Tessa added.

"Maybe they moved away," Patrick said. "Maybe they were too sad here."

"Maybe," Will said.

"At least Emaline is buried with her brothers and sister, not like Adam. He had to be buried with strangers all around."

Tessa smiled down at Patrick. "You're right, Patrick. I guess I didn't think of it that way."

"I wonder whatever happened to Brennan," Patrick said.

"And the captain and Martha . . ." Will added.

"And Polly and Pearl and Prudence and Mae," Patrick said wistfully. "And I wonder if . . ."

Will, figuring that Patrick was going to start talking about the long-lost Murdock again, hopped on his bike. "C'mon," he said, "we've still got chores to do."

"Can you stop back at my house for just a minute?" Tessa asked as they neared her turnoff.

"Sure," Will said, "but we'll have to hurry."

Tessa parked her bike and headed for the little brick house by the garden. She went around to the back corner, stopped and counted five bricks down, then ten bricks over. The loose brick slid out easily, revealing a small cavity. Tessa took the ring off, wrapped it in a small square of dark blue cloth she'd found in her mother's sewing basket, and placed it in the hole. She pushed the brick back in and dusted her hands on the seat of her jeans.

"It doesn't belong to me," she said. "It belongs to another time."

Will nodded and turned to go. Suddenly Margie and Barley, barking wildly, sped off toward the canal. By the time the kids caught up with them, the dogs had disappeared into a clump of cattails. Patrick ran ahead to see what the dogs had cornered.

"Watch it, Patrick," Will warned. "It might be a skunk."

Patrick carefully parted the reeds. A happy yapping joined with Margie's high-pitched barks and Barley's deep mellow woofs. A second later, a yellow blur burst out of the cattails and flung itself on Patrick, knocking the boy flat on his back. It was a half-grown pup who wriggled all over, whining in delight.

"Murdock!" Patrick cried as the dog washed his face with a wide, pink tongue.

"Murdock!" Tessa and Will yelled in unison. Mouths hanging open, they stared wide-eyed and speechless at each other, then at Patrick and the dog.

"Good ol' Murdock!" Patrick said, hugging the wiggling puppy. "I knew he'd find his way home. All he had to do was follow the canal!"